# DISCOVERED OBSESSION

# DISCOVERED OBSESSION

THE DISCOVERED TRUTH SERIES ROMANTIC
SUSPENSE
BOOK TWELVE

JULIE BAWDEN DAVIS

Roses
ARE
RED
PUBLISHING

Copyright © 2021 Roses are Red Publishing

All rights reserved.

Cover by Judy Bullard (customebookcovers.com)

Book design by Julie Bawden-Davis

Palm logo design by Kayla Curry

Roses are Red logo design by Kyle Kane

This is a work of fiction. Characters and incidents are the product of the author's imagination. Any perceived likenesses are coincidental.

ISBN 13: 978-1-955265-34-8

ISBN 10: 1-955265-34-8

Distributed by Roses Are Red Publishing

rosesareredpublishing.com

❀ Created with Vellum

# ACKNOWLEDGMENTS

As they say, it takes a village. Here's my village. I'm supremely grateful to each of these fabulous people!

**ARC Reading Gems**
Julie Schlueter
Tara Bradley
Susa Fraccaroli
Kery Bailey
Trish Darrenkamp
Marilyn Smith
Lisa Starkey
Heather Wamboldt
Monte Bawden
Beth Helm
Teresa Reitnauer
Chelle Young
Asra Syed
Jacquelyn Gray
Amber Mancebo

**Pros**
Sharon Whatley, editing
Judy Bullard, cover design
Kayla Curry, logo design
Kyle Kane, logo design
Sabrina Wildermuth, design consultation
Jeremy Davis, technical support

*To Lupe, whose journey to America was fraught with its own perils.*

# PROLOGUE

The room was small and stuffy, the paper-thin curtains shifted listlessly in the slight breeze. Neighbor children had lined up outside the apartment, straining to see into the room. Her brow covered in sweat, her eyes bright, the teenage girl screamed as she pushed, then grasped her mother's hand. The older woman stood next to her daughter and bent down to whisper in her ear, "Shh, *lánya*, the *baba* is almost here."

The midwife returned with a metal bowl of water and saw a little boy's nose pressed up against the glass. She shrieked, *"Menj innen!"* The children scurried away, tittering as they did.

After dipping a rag into the water and squeezing it out, the midwife handed it to the mother, who used the cloth to gently stroke her daughter's brow.

Then the midwife went to the foot of the small bed and eased the girl's legs farther apart. She inserted her fingers and felt, then urged, "Push."

The girl responded by bearing down. As she did so, her hands clenched so hard on her mother's hand that she drew blood with her fingernails as a searing pain ripped through her abdominal region. She felt a sucking sensation as the baby left her body and her abdomen distended. The midwife worked quickly to cut the cord. Then she raised the baby to her shoulder and slapped the tiny body on the back until a high-pitched cry filled the room.

The mother and daughter smiled in relief as the woman put the baby on an old wooden table and dipped a clean cloth into the water. She used it to carefully wipe out the baby's eyes and nose and ears, then cleaned the rest of her body, checking her fingers and toes as she did so. After wrapping the baby in a worn blanket, she handed her to the mother and said, "The *baba* needs to eat. After you feed her, I'll take her to the orphanage."

The baby had started eagerly suckling, and the girl stroked the fuzzy brown hair on her head.

Her mother stood taller and faced the midwife. "We are going to keep her."

"That's not wise. It will be a hard life for your daughter and the baby. Are you sure?"

The mother looked to her daughter, who nodded her head, her eyes already full of love and awe for her flesh and blood.

"Very well," said the midwife as she went to tend to the afterbirth.

When she left, the mother took the sleeping baby from her daughter's breast and announced, "Alexandra Aliz Farkas. We shall call her Sasha."

# PRESENT DAY

## LOS ANGELES, CALIFORNIA

Hans Wagner entered his last patient's room and asked, "*Señor* Martinez, how are you feeling? *Cómo está usted?*"

The man chuckled. "I see that your Spanish accent hasn't improved since the last time I saw you, doctor."

Hans gave the older man a mock expression of affront, then replied, "Thank goodness my surgical skills are better."

"*Sí.*" The man smiled.

Hans consulted the computer next to the bed and pulled up his chart. *Señor* Martinez's EEG showed promising results, as well as the MRI. He checked another screen. Liver function was back to normal.

Hans walked to the head of the bed and shined his penlight into each of the man's eyes, then carefully checked the stitched incision under the bandage on his head. "I've got some good news for you. All your test results are excellent today."

The man appeared hopeful. "You're saying that I am *mejor*?

Hans smiled. "*Mucho mejor.* The tumor removal was a success. You'll be back to your old self within a month or so."

The man looked relieved. "*Gracias*, Doctor."

"No need to thank me, *Señor* Martinez, it's my job. Get some rest now." Hans made some notes in the computer, then logged off and left the room.

In the men's locker room, Hans dialed his combination and opened his locker. Then he stripped out of his blue scrubs and stuffed them in his laundry bag and pulled out his street clothes—jeans and a black t-shirt.

"I'd ask if you have a hot date, but I know better," said Chuck Cooper, a young internist who was prematurely balding. He yanked a backpack out of his locker and slung it over his shoulder.

Hans's colleagues at Mercy General liked to rib him about the fact that he always dressed before leaving the hospital, rather than walking out in scrubs. He stepped into the jeans, buttoning them, and pulled his t-shirt over his head, then slipped his bare feet into a pair of loafers. "What if I told you I do have a hot date?"

Chuck turned to him with a grin. "The nurse in critical care?"

"I'm meeting my mother at her assisted living facility for lunch."

Chuck snorted and rolled his eyes. "Why did I bother asking?"

The two men walked out of the hospital into the hot August midday sun. Chuck kept walking but Hans stopped when he saw a black sedan at the far side of the parking lot—the same one he'd seen when he started his shift.

"Scalpel, please. And check the patient's vitals again."

Sasha Farkas handed the doctor the scalpel, then read off the monitor. "Her BP is 150 over 80 and holding. Heart rate is slightly elevated."

Dr. Cesero nodded, then he went back to work on the patient's face. A woman from Brazil who wasn't happy with the chin implant another doctor had given her. Sasha watched, puzzled as always by the quest for perfection. Her own face was less than perfect, and she liked it that way. A cosmetic surgeon would probably want to remove the small heart shaped mole on Sasha's left cheek and perhaps shorten her nose. But it was her face. She wondered how odd it must feel to look in the mirror and see someone else. Then she reminded herself that it was thanks to people's pursuit of perfection that she had a job here in America.

When the procedure was complete four hours later, Sasha scrubbed up at the sink. It had been a long week of assisting at more procedures than her tired brain could possibly count. She looked forward to going home for the night.

As she was about to leave, the last patient began crying out. Sasha went to the woman's room to find Dr. Cesero assuring her that the pain medicine would kick in soon. When his cellphone buzzed, he turned to Sasha. "Go to the service elevator. A patient is being brought in. Tell the transport person you're standing in for me because I've got an emergency, then bring the patient here."

Sasha nodded and walked through the silent halls of the med-surg center until she arrived at the gleaming main elevator. She pushed the basement level button and entered. As the elevator headed into the bowels of the building, she thought about how this was the first time she'd been sent down here to retrieve a patient. Generally, Dr. Cesero or

JULIE BAWDEN DAVIS

Antonio made the pickup. She usually didn't see the person until they were on the operating table. Her stomach felt uneasy when she got out and headed down the empty corridor to the service elevator. It wasn't long before the elevator groaned to life and came rattling down to the basement. As the doors slid open, Sasha came face-to-face with a burly man in a black suit. He had an unconscious young woman in a wheelchair in tow. Surprise registered on his face when he saw Sasha. Then he reached into a holster under his jacket and pulled out a gun.

## 2

Sasha raised her hands and said, "I'm Dr. Cesero's nurse. He's dealing with an emergency, so he sent me." She eyed the woman in the wheelchair.

The man checked behind her in the corridor, then re-holstered his gun. "Okay, take her."

Sasha hesitated.

"I said take her," the man growled. He had unruly dark hair and an unshaven face.

Sasha lowered her arms but kept her eyes on the man, who pushed the wheelchair out of the elevator toward her. She reached for the woman's arm and quickly checked her pulse. Weak. Then she slowly went around to the back of the chair before beginning to push the woman down the hall to the office elevator. The man followed a few steps behind as Sasha moved deliberately, keenly aware of the gun under his jacket. When they got to the elevator, the door opened immediately. Sasha saw from the corner of her eye the man's shoulders visibly relax when he saw no one was inside. She pushed the wheelchair into the elevator and turned it around. As they traveled up to the medical center, the woman moaned slightly. Sasha put her hands on the sides of her arms in silent reassurance.

When the elevator doors opened, Dr. Cesero was waiting to greet them. "Nurse Farkas get our patient into room three. I'll take a look at her immediately."

As Sasha wheeled the woman into the room, she heard Dr. Cesero talking to the man in a low voice.

Just then their orderly, Antonio, came in. "The doctor wants her on the table," he announced. He had the short, wiry build of a lightweight boxer, but Sasha knew from experience watching him move patients that he was strong.

As Antonio lowered the hospital table and lifted the woman up and onto it, Sasha took a good look at her for the first time. She was most likely mid-twenties and wore a lightweight cerulean blue dress. Her feet were bare, her toenails polished pink. Her jet-black hair was dark against pale skin.

Dr. Cesero came in shouting orders. "Start an IV with fluids, nurse. We need to flush her system. Antonio, I need you to stay tonight. I'm going to pump her stomach." He checked the woman's pupils, then opened her mouth and shined a flashlight inside. "Two milligrams of Naloxone," he instructed. "If she doesn't improve within five minutes, give her two more."

Then Dr. Cesero left the room. Right before the door swung shut, Sasha saw the man with the gun waiting to talk to him.

"Your child is well, but you are not, Mrs. Farkas. Did you take the vitamins I gave you last month?"

Sasha, eight at the time, watched as her *Anya's* thin face reddened. Then her mother gazed down at the floor of the medical center in Budapest, as if the tiles would give her an answer. The smell of alcohol wafted their way as a baby in the adjacent cubicle began wailing. Shots, thought Sasha. She was glad to be done with them.

When her mother still didn't reply, Sasha blurted, "*Anya* traded the vitamins for a winter coat for me." She held her breath and waited for her mother's reply.

The doctor, a woman from America with gray, frizzy hair and glasses hanging from a chain around her neck, sighed. "Mrs. Farkas, if you aren't well, you can't properly care for your daughter. The vitamins are a gift from UNICEF to help you. I'm going to give you another bottle, but you must promise me you'll take them."

Sasha's mother raised her head, her eyes earnest as she said, "I will take them, doctor. Thank you."

The doctor smiled, then reached down to ruffle Sasha's hair. "Do you like your new winter coat?" she asked, the stethoscope around her neck catching Sasha's eye as it glinted in the light.

"It has pockets," Sasha answered.

The doctor laughed. "Pockets are always good."

Sasha agreed, thinking how it gave her a place to slip things she found in the trash on her way home from school.

Hans pulled up in front of Meadowbrook Village and

parked his Volvo. Then he took the bouquet he'd bought and strolled to the front door.

At the reception desk, he greeted Yvonne, a pert, young woman with a bright smile. "Dr. Wagner. What lovely roses."

"Please call me Hans, Yvonne. Is my mother in the dining hall?"

"She is. Have a good visit."

Hans walked down the carpeted hallway toward the clatter of dishes. When he entered the cavernous room lit by giant chandeliers, he scanned the diners for his mother's table. He spotted her talking to another woman, their heads together.

He was a few feet from the table when his mother looked up and exclaimed, "Hans, please sit. Have you met my friend, Gloria? Her daughter, Josephine, will be joining us for lunch."

"Very nice to meet you, Gloria," he said. Then he handed his mother the flowers.

"These are beautiful, Hans," his mother beamed. "See, what I mean?" she said to her friend. "He is the best son."

Gloria, a jowly woman with bifocals perched on the end of her nose, nodded. "Good sons are hard to come by." She gave Hans the once-over as he sat down, his back to the doorway.

"Tell me," his mother said more loudly than necessary. "Whose life did you save today?"

Hans picked up his cloth napkin and set it on his lap. "I'm afraid my rounds were uneventful," he replied. "How has your day been, ladies?"

His mother threw her hand back. "Oh, you know, the usual. Mr. Pickering tried to cheat at bingo, and I caught him." She stopped talking and looked beyond Hans toward the dining hall entrance.

"Yoo-hoo, Josie, over here!" Gloria called out as she waved.

Hans turned to see a woman dressed in a yellow flowing pantsuit sauntering toward them. When she reached the table, she leaned down to plant a kiss on Gloria's cheek, leaving behind red lipstick.

"This is my friend Gretchen," said Gloria to the woman, "and her son, Hans, the doctor. My daughter, Josephine," she proclaimed. "She's a model."

Hans stood and took her hand. "Very nice to meet you," he said.

"Likewise," Josephine answered.

Then they both sat down.

Hans pretended to look over the day's menu while keeping Josephine in his periphery. This was a first for his mother. Though she often mentioned his single status, she had never resorted to matchmaking.

## 3

Hans pushed his mother's wheelchair back to her room, the silence between them weighing the mood. "Do you want me to help you into bed for a nap? Or will you stay up?" he asked.

More silence, his mother's downturned mouth grim with disapproval.

"I'll take that as you want to stay in your chair." Hans pushed her next to the window and in view of her television set. He noted that someone had put the bouquet of tiny pink roses and baby's breath he'd brought her in a vase and set it on the bedside table.

"You could have at least made an effort," his mother said finally.

Hans jangled his car keys in his pocket. "Josephine is a beautiful woman. We just didn't have a lot to say to one another. The world of modeling is something I know nothing about."

His mother threw up her hands. "Who says you have to have something in common! Your father and I had nothing in common, and we were happily married for forty years."

"That was a different time, Mom. Look, I know you want grandchildren. That's what this is about, isn't it?"

The indignation on his mother's round face eased up. "Edith Graverstein's grandchildren come to visit her every Saturday. I hear them next door. It's just…" She took ahold of the silver locket that hung around her neck with the photo of her, Hans, and his father tucked inside. "I get so lonely."

A wave of sadness swept through Hans as the face of his father filled his head. He knelt next to his mother and took her hand. "I know it's hard without Dad. How about I come on my next day off and we watch one of your favorite movies together?"

His mother smiled. "Gone with the Wind?"

Hans laughed. "I can't promise I'll make it through the whole four hours, but fine, yes, we'll watch it."

She let go of the locket and squeezed his hands. "You're a good son. Forgive me for trying to run your life. I get carried away sometimes."

Hans kissed her powder soft cheek. "It shows how much you care."

"The patient appears to be stabilizing," said Dr. Cesero, nodding in approval. "I think you can go home, Nurse Farkas."

Sasha started to leave the room, when he added, "It goes without saying that you didn't see any of this." He lowered his head and looked at her over the top of his glasses. "You understand?"

Sasha took a deep breath, then nodded. "Perfectly. What time would you like me back in the morning, doctor?"

"Make it seven a.m."

Sasha walked down the empty hallway, then got into the elevator and took it to the bottom floor and lobby. She pushed open the double doors to the parking lot where she started up her old, silver Honda and headed out of the lot and toward home. Ten minutes later, she pulled into her apartment complex in Los Angeles and locked her car, then hurried to her door. The neighborhood was fairly safe, but she'd learned from experience that if something bad was going to happen, it was going to happen in the middle of the night. Once inside her studio apartment, she sighed with relief. After securing the two deadbolts she'd installed herself, she went to the kitchen and took a carton of orange juice out of the refrigerator. She poured herself a small glass and drank several sips. After removing her sneakers and stripping off her scrubs and depositing them in the hamper, she sat down on the edge of the bed and pulled open her nightstand drawer, removing a small notebook. She flipped to the last page of entries and eyed the balance. $6,700. With next week's paycheck, after paying her bills and sending her mother money, she would have $6,750. She still had a long way to go to buy her freedom.

"*Anya*, please, drink the milk. It's fresh from Mrs. Balik's goat. It will help make you strong again." Sasha was twelve at the time, and they were in their one-bedroom apartment in

Budapest. Her mother was in bed with pneumonia. Lack of food hindered her recovery.

Her mother shook her head. "No. For you."

"Mrs. Balik gave me plenty of milk. My belly is full. This is for you. If I must, I will pour it down your throat." Sasha felt the familiar frustration and anxiety fill her chest. "Please, *Anya*." She leaned down and brushed her mother's cheek with her own, then whispered, "I don't want you to leave me alone."

Her mother's hazel eyes softened, and she opened her mouth. Relief sweeping through her, Sasha slowly dribbled the liquid into her mouth, waiting between each small swallow before giving her more. Once the milk was gone, Sasha reached for the bag of apples Mrs. Balik had given her. She would cut them up and make applesauce. Her mother loved applesauce.

As Sasha prepared the apples for cooking, she thought about what she had done for the food. She had cleaned out the Balik's pigsty. Mrs. Balik wasn't so bad. But her husband filled Sasha with disgust. He always watched her with a dirty look in his eyes and brushed himself up against her whenever he could. Today, when she was rinsing the pig slop off herself in the hose, she had spotted him watching her. Shuddering at the memory, she nearly nicked her finger with the knife. She shook her head to clear the vile image and focused on the apples. Before long, the sweet smell of cooking fruit filled the air.

"You look like you're feeling better, *Anya*, compared to a just few minutes ago," said Sasha when the fruit was done. "I have some applesauce for us."

"I am feeling better. I must have needed that milk. I didn't ask you, how was your day?"

Sasha came to her mother with the fragrant applesauce piled into an earthenware bowl, an old metal spoon in her hand. "It was wonderful," she lied. "The woman is having me take care of her *baba*. I bounced him on my knee."

Her mother smiled and reached out to pat Sasha's arm. "So much work for a young girl. I will be well soon and go back to sewing. Then you can focus on your studies."

Sasha took a spoonful of applesauce and lifted it toward her mother's mouth. She fully intended to focus on her studies and one day become a nurse. Then she could keep her *Anya* well, and they would never go without food.

# 4

Sasha woke to the alarm sounding in her ear, her heart pounding at being interrupted from a deep, although brief sleep. She had just thirty minutes to get back to the medical center. She pulled open her bedside drawer and reached for her mother's recent letter. Unfolding the lined notebook paper, she read:

*Sasha, do not worry about me. I am well. Thank you for the money. I am so proud of you. A nurse in America. God willing, we will see each other one day soon.*

*Szeretet,*

*Anya*

Sasha gently refolded the letter and put it back in the drawer. In the bathroom, she pushed her hair back and splashed her face with cold water, then brushed her teeth. After pulling on clean scrubs and her nursing shoes, she went into the small kitchen to brew herself a cup of coffee. Then she lifted a banana from the fruit bowl and unpeeled it. As she ate a piece of the sweet, ripe fruit, she thought about the patient from last night. Sasha never asked questions at the clinic, but that didn't stop her from wondering. Would the young woman still be there when she got back? Who was she?

At the table, she unplugged her phone from the charger and powered it on, then went to the search bar and pulled up the *Los Angeles Times* website. She skimmed the headlines for anything that might tell her who the young woman was. Nothing. But one headline caught her eye: *ICE Raids East LA Free Clinic.* Her heart performing acrobatics in her chest, she read how immigration authorities had swept the clinic for illegal immigrants. Her anxiety eased when she learned no employees had been pinpointed as illegals, but the fact that they were raiding clinics disturbed her. She decided not to finish her morning coffee. She was fully awake now.

Hans turned off the treadmill, then wiped the sweat from his face and headed for the bathroom. He'd been in his condo only a few months, but already felt better about not throwing money away on rent. He still had a substantial student loan to pay off for medical school, and his financial advisor had convinced him that the money saved with a tax write-off from home ownership would help him pay it off faster. The condo was in West Hollywood and within walking distance of the hospital, although like many Angelenos, he usually drove.

He opened the refrigerator and longed for a leisurely breakfast of scrambled eggs and toast, an entire pot of fresh coffee along with the newspaper, but instead took out a protein drink. While standing there, he drank down half, then checked the clock. Just enough time to shower and get back to the hospital.

"Nurse Farkas, there you are," said Dr. Cesero when Sasha walked into the patient's room. The woman appeared to still be unconscious. "Let's hope she comes around soon," he said just as there was a loud sound in the hallway. Eyes wide, he turned toward the door. "Stay here with her. I want to know the moment there is any change in her vitals."

Sasha nodded as the doctor left the room and shut the door. She strained to hear what was occurring in the hallway. A man's voice, and he sounded angry. She couldn't make much out, but what she did understand sounded like threats. It was clear they were speaking of the young woman.

Taking the woman's hand in hers, Sasha checked the monitor. Though some medical professionals might chide her for being unscientific, she believed with all her heart that the unconscious could hear. "You must wake up," she whispered. "I don't know who you are, but you are young, and you are strong." Sasha continued to hold the woman's hand, glancing at the monitor as she did so. She jumped when she heard a raised voice in the hallway and Dr. Cesero crying out. Then there came a sudden thump and the sound of boots marching away. Sasha walked quietly to the door. She stood there, holding her breath. She could hear a man's ragged breathing. Was that Dr. Cesero? Sasha reached for the handle when she heard someone else approach. It sounded like high heels.

"Oh, my god, Nathaniel. I saw Petrov's man leaving. What

did he do to you? Let me help you up." Sasha knew that voice. It was Alina.

"Just give me a moment," Sasha heard Dr. Cesero mumble.

"I take it she didn't regain consciousness?" said Alina in a low voice.

"I've got the nurse in with her, but she's unresponsive. We need a specialist."

"I'm working on that," Alina blurted. "I've got someone in mind. I just need a little more time."

"If we don't get her awake soon, we're all dead."

"For god's sake," said Alina, "what is his obsession with that woman?"

"All I know is that he's ready to kill to keep her alive." Dr. Cesero groaned. "Don't mind me, but I'm not ready to die."

Sasha's stomach clenched at his words, and she feared what she had become a party to. Whoever the man was, he meant business. The girl was connected in some fearful and very dangerous way. Sasha suddenly felt confined in the room and wished she could leave and go home. But she would never abandon a patient. She walked across the room to the window and looked down into the parking lot. No one was around, but she worried it was only a matter of time until the man returned.

"What have you gotten yourself into?" she said to the patient, smoothing her hair from her face. It sounded to Sasha as if Dr. Cesero had no way out. And if the woman died. Then what? Would they come after Sasha, too? Goosebumps pricked across her skin.

## 5

Hans checked the clinical data on one last patient chart and signed off. It had been a long twelve-hour shift, and he wanted nothing more than to go home, grab a beer, and stop thinking. He walked down the hall and stopped at the critical care desk. A nurse, whose name escaped him now, looked up from the computer screen.

"I just checked on Mr. Henderson in room 5, Nurse Martin," Hans said, his recall kicking in. "Keep close track of his blood pressure. The Chlorthalidone I prescribed earlier this evening should start doing its job."

The woman was pretty and very pleasant, and from her usual attentiveness to every detail of his day, Hans wondered if she might be interested. But he barely had the time and energy, and it would end up only being a date or two, anyway.

"Are you off now, Dr. Wagner?" Small dimples presented themselves on both cheeks when she smiled.

"I am. Dr. Phelps should be in soon. I hope the floor stays quiet the rest of the night. Have a good evening."

"The same to you." She went back to her computer.

After changing from his scrubs and into sweatpants and a shirt, he headed to the side exit and his car. Though it was just after midnight, the temperature still hovered around eighty degrees. He would need the air conditioner tonight. As he approached his parking spot, he hesitated, wary. Someone was sitting in the passenger side of his car. He pulled his cellphone out of his pocket, ready to dial 911, while he approached cautiously. "What are you doing in my car?" he asked loudly, staying back several feet.

The car door opened and a woman wearing sunglasses and a scarf on her head pointed a gun at him. "Your services are needed, Dr. Wagner," she said. "Get in the car."

Hans backed up. "What the hell? I'm not going anywhere."

"Your mother, Gretchen, lives in an assisted living facility in Sherman Oaks. It would be a shame if she didn't wake up in the morning."

An icy sliver of fear ran down Hans's spine. He put his cellphone back in his pocket and walked toward the driver's side and got in.

Sasha sat next to the woman's bed watching her breathing, slow and steady. She checked her vitals and wrote the numbers on a clipboard. Part of Sasha wanted to see if she might be responsive, but instead she checked her IV drip, then busied herself rearranging her pillow and smoothing the covers.

The door opened and Dr. Cesero walked in. He was a tall man with a full head of black hair and usually appeared well-groomed and rested. Tonight, though, his eyes were bloodshot and expression gloomy. His appearance told her that his comment about them all being in trouble if this woman didn't wake up was more than an idle threat.

"No change," she murmured, then handed him the chart. He checked the numbers and shook his head, clipping it to the end of the bed. His cellphone buzzed then, and he checked the screen. "You can go now, Nurse Farkas. I'll see you tomorrow morning."

Surprised to be relieved with the patient situation as it was, Sasha wasn't about to argue. "Okay, doctor. I changed her IV about an hour ago."

He sat down in the chair Sasha had vacated and gave her a quick nod, then scooted to the edge of his chair, intent now on the woman's breathing.

Sasha decided to leave before he changed his mind, quietly closing the door behind her. After grabbing her purse and a water bottle out of the break-room, she walked down the hallway toward the elevator. She hoped that a miracle would occur overnight, and she'd come back in the morning to see the woman awake and sitting up in bed.

When she got in the elevator, Sasha was surprised that the button for the lobby was already lit. Who could be here at this hour, she wondered? The door slid open when Sasha reached the bottom floor, and there stood Alina and a man. He appeared as startled to see Sasha as she was to see him.

"You're excused," Alina said to Sasha, gesturing for her to get out of the elevator. Sasha exited, and as she did so, peeked up quickly at the man, whose eyes were a deep blue and looked as anxious as Sasha felt. As she walked to the front door, her head down, Sasha heard the elevator close. She turned quickly to see that the destination was Dr. Cesero's floor.

Hans had been surprised to see someone in the elevator at this hour. The woman, a striking brunette, wore blue scrubs. When he watched her walk out of the elevator and toward the exit, the redhead said, "I advise that you forget everything and everyone you see here." She had removed her scarf and the sunglasses to reveal aquiline features and gray eyes that showed no emotion. Her red hair was combed back severely and wrapped into a tight bun on the back of her head.

When Hans eyed her scarf and sunglasses, she commented, "Too many cameras at the hospital."

After the elevator came to a stop on the third floor, the doors opened to a suite. "To the right and straight down the hall," she ordered him as they walked past the empty reception desk. When they arrived at a door with a 3 on the front, she knocked and called out, "He's here."

A man in a physician's coat opened the door and looked from the woman to Hans.

"This is Dr. Hans Wagner," she said. "Neurosurgeon at Mercy General."

The man nodded approvingly. "I'll take it from here. Why don't you check on our delivery?"

Hans looked over the man's shoulder to see a young woman in a hospital bed.

"Twenty-five-year-old female who appears to have over-dosed," the man said.

"And you are?" Hans asked.

"My name is Nathaniel Cesero, and I am a physician. Now, please, take a look at the patient."

Hans hesitated now that his gun-carrying escort had disappeared. But the young woman clearly needed more medical attention than she was receiving. He went over and checked her pupils, then consulted the clipboard hanging from the end of the bed. "You gave her Naloxone and pumped her stomach. Did anyone administer epinephrine?"

"No," said Cesero. "Would that have been indicated?"

"Only if she was allergic to whatever she ingested. Which was what, do you know?"

Cesero sighed. "I don't know."

"Do you have an EEG machine?" asked Hans.

"Actually, I have one being delivered momentarily."

Hans glanced around the room. "What does this medical center specialize in? Are you a general practitioner?"

The comment seemed to annoy the man, who huffed, "Certainly not. I'm a plastic surgeon."

Before Hans could reply, the redhead pushed an EEG machine into the room.

"That is a high-end model," Hans noted. "I should be able to get some answers."

"There are no shoulds, Dr. Wagner. You must," said Cesero.

# 6

Hans measured the unconscious woman's head, then smoothed down her dark hair and carefully attached electrodes. What if the answer he got was that the woman was brain dead? He didn't trust these people and feared what might happen next. Even if her condition had nothing to do with Hans, they would probably kill him—their insurance against secrets concerning the woman from getting out. His pulse raced at the thought.

As Hans worked, Cesero and the redhead left the room to confer in the hallway. Their voices carried but it wasn't anything Hans could make out. At one point, the woman's voice became almost shrill.

When Hans had all the electrodes attached, he went to the computer control box and entered in as much data as he could about the woman, guessing at her weight. Then he started the machine to record any evidence of brain activity.

An hour later, Hans had sufficient data from the readout to analyze the patient's brain function. What Hans saw was promising, and he expelled his fear in one long, nervous breath.

"Well?" said the redhead, who came into the room with Cesero just then.

Hans hugged his arms across his chest and replied, "The good news is that she has brain activity. The overdose doesn't appear to have caused any long-term damage."

"What's the bad news?" asked the doctor.

"She is currently in a coma. Which suggests her brain is protecting itself for some reason. It may just be that the trauma from the overdose was too taxing, and her system needs time to recuperate."

"How much time?" asked the redhead.

"The next twenty-four hours are critical. If she comes out of the coma within that time frame, and her brain function continues to seem healthy, we can consider her survival highly likely."

A strained tension hung in the air.

"And if twenty-four hours pass?" asked Cesero. Hans watched the man's body language, how his shoulders hunched forward, as if the thought of attack lie just below the surface.

"Then she could have some brain damage that the EEG hasn't picked up, which could indicate she has lost some body function." At the look of panic in Cesero's eyes, Hans backpedaled. "There's a good chance she will wake up in the next few hours. I wouldn't be surprised if she's walking around tomorrow."

"What else do we need to do to make sure she stays functioning?" asked the redhead.

Hans thought for a moment. "Research suggests that if you talk to people in a coma, they do hear you. Someone close to the patient would be more likely to have a positive impact."

"Then make sure you do just that while attending to her," the woman said to Hans.

"I need to get back to the hospital in a few hours. If I don't show up for my next shift, someone will notice that I'm missing."

The redhead looked at Cesero and raised her eyebrows.

"You will stay here until our nurse returns in the morning," Cesero said to Hans. "We'll wheel in a cot for you. I don't need to remind you that your mother's life hangs in the balance. You should know by now that I won't hesitate to carry out my threat."

As Sasha lay in bed willing herself to sleep, the face of the man she'd seen in the elevator ran through her mind. Who was he, she wondered? She glanced at the clock and sighed. She had very little time before going back to the clinic. Frustrated, she got up and went to the kitchen to warm herself a mug of milk. At the table, she sipped the hot drink and opened the notepad she used to write letters to her mother. She reached for a pen and started a new letter.

*Anya,*

*Thank you for your recent letter. I am so glad to hear you are doing better and that the nurses are taking good care of you. I am doing very well. My job is very busy, but I am helping many sick people. I especially love helping the children. They smile when I give them candy after the doctor gives them their shots.*

*The prices here in America are very high, so I am sorry I wasn't able to send you the extra money I promised last month. I have paid for your care this month, and some extra is enclosed. Please buy a warm sweater for the winter. It will be cold soon in Hungary.*

*You asked what the weather is like here in Los Angeles. It is warm and sunny most days. On my days off, sometimes I go to the beach to think of you and home. I am sprinkling some sand in the envelope so that you have something I have touched here in America.*

*I know you wish for me to come home soon for a visit. I am not sure that is possible, but I will do my best.*

*Szeretlek,*

*Sasha*

Sasha got the jar of sand she had managed to gather at the beach the other night when she finished working before a lifeguard came by in his jeep to tell her the beach was closed. She took out a glue stick and ran a sticky line across the bottom of the letter. After sprinkling sand on the glue and pressing it into the paper, she left it out to dry.

When she went back to bed, she felt calmer. She might not be with her mother, but writing to her—even if it was mostly untruths—made her feel closer to her. Her mother was so proud of her. Sasha couldn't tell her the truth. That she was being forced to help a plastic surgeon with a bunch of silly, rich patients, and that she still had a long way to go before she paid him and his colleagues off for her passage to America. They had promised once she worked off her debt to them that she'd get her green card. Sasha longed for that day.

"Sasha, you are going to America?" her mother asked, her face stricken. "I thought you wanted a job here in a hospital?"

Sasha had graduated from nursing school nine months before but hadn't been able to find any work in Budapest. When a friend told her about a man interested in talking to Hungarian professionals about working in America, she jumped at the chance. He said his company was a placement agency and would provide airfare, a passport, even a place to stay once she arrived.

"I don't know about this," her mother said, her breathing becoming labored. "Natalya's daughter left for America six months ago, and no one has heard from her."

"I will be fine, *Anya*," she assured her mother, while not feeling all that sure herself. "The man said they need nurses in America. I will make money I can send you. You can finally go to the treatment facility, and they can heal your lungs."

Her mother considered. "You promise me you will be okay, and that you will come back for visits?"

"I promise," said Sasha, hoping she could live up to the faith she saw in her mother's eyes.

## 7

When Cesero and the redhead seemed to have retired for the night, Hans took the opportunity to make a call to his mother's care facility.

"She's sleeping peacefully, Dr. Wagner," the nurse on duty assured him.

"She hasn't had any visitors?" he asked, trying to sound nonchalant.

"Visitors? No. Was she expecting someone?"

"An old family friend said he might be in the neighborhood, but it looks like he didn't stop by. Let me know if anyone does."

"Of course. Anything else?"

"Nothing. Thank you for checking on her."

"You're welcome, and goodnight."

Hans breathed a sigh of relief that his mother appeared to be okay and hadn't had any strange visitors. He went to check on the unconscious woman. "I don't know who you are," he said, standing over her bed, "but your fate appears to be tied to mine, so I'd really appreciate you waking up now." He stared at her motionless face, then checked her reflexes, which were good. Suddenly, the woman moaned, and Hans leaned closer. He watched her eyes move rapidly beneath her eyelids. But she remained unconscious.

Sasha arrived at the office building just as the sun was coming up. She peered through the glass doors to see the janitor emptying a trash can. He was a short man with a bald head and a slight pot belly. The door was locked, so she tapped on it with her car key. When he saw who it was, he came toward the door and greeted her with a smile. "You're in early," he said as he pulled the door open.

"A lot of work today," she replied over her shoulder as she headed to the elevator, where she pushed the up arrow to Dr. Cesero's floor. As she waited, she wondered if the young woman had awakened yet. Sasha had never seen Dr. Cesero so anxious about a patient.

When she knocked on the office door five minutes later, Alina opened it and stared at Sasha coldly. She wore black pants and a steel-gray silk blouse and her signature high heels. "Early. I like that. Dr. Cesero will be in soon. We have another doctor on duty right now. He's going to update you on the patient's progress."

Sasha nodded, then followed Alina down the hallway. She had worked here for three years now and had never seen any other doctors or nurses. Sasha and Dr. Cesero worked alone, with Antonio usually coming in during after-hours to clean up.

When Alina pushed the door to the young woman's room open, Sasha was surprised to see the man from the elevator.

He wore a physician's coat over the sweatpants and shirt she'd seen him in last night. When their eyes met, he gave her a quick smile that enlivened his face.

"The patient appears to be better," he said to Alina, who went to her bedside.

"How can you tell?" she asked.

"I did another EEG, and there is a change in brainwave activity that indicates she'll be making her way out of the coma soon."

"How soon?"

"Within the next twelve hours or so."

"When she does, give her a thorough examination."

The doctor glanced at his watch. "Very soon, I'm expected at the hospital."

"Come back after your shift. Give any instructions to the nurse." She turned on her heels and left the room.

After the door shut, Sasha looked over at the doctor, his eyes on her, and suddenly felt shy.

He smiled. "I'm Hans Wagner. You are?"

Sasha waited a moment to speak, afraid she might trip over her words and make a fool of herself. "Nurse Farkas," she said, looking down at her feet and up into his face again.

He cocked his head to one side. "You have an accent. You're not from here?"

Anxiety tightened in Sasha's chest. "No, but I have my nursing license."

He frowned. "I didn't mean anything by that. My mother is German, so I notice accents. Is it Romanian?"

Sasha hesitated. Was this a trick? Had the man been sent from ICE?

He shook his head. "Never mind. I'm prying. Let me update you on our patient."

Sasha felt the tension in her chest ease when he abandoned the subject and went on to tell her about the woman's condition and what she needed to do. It was all standard, except for talking to the patient, which Sasha had already been doing.

As Hans spoke, he couldn't help noticing how flawless the nurse's skin was, and she wore little if no makeup. Her brown hair hung down her back in a thick braid, and she had on scrubs that he could tell had been ironed. Though he was warm with her, her expression remained watchful and serious, almost strained. She nodded often and only spoke when necessary. Given what he'd seen in this place so far, Hans wondered what she had experienced as a nurse here.

## 8

Sasha listened as the doctor filled her in on the patient but had a hard time focusing on his words. She was struck by his kind, gentle manner. He treated her like she was a real person. That was an attitude Sasha hadn't seen much of in her three years as a nurse. When he spoke, his eyes met hers, and he listened when she answered.

"Would you like to see the two EEG results to give this a bit more context?" he asked.

Sasha nodded vigorously, and he laughed, which made her face flush. He quickly said, "I'm not laughing at you. I'm just happy someone is interested in what I have to say and not bored by it. He pulled up the EEG machine and tapped in some information, then motioned for her to come stand next to him. Sasha did so, suddenly aware he was taller than she first thought, broad shouldered. Standing inches from him, she noticed a pleasant musky scent.

"This is the first test," he said, pointing to various lines on a graph on the screen. He pushed a button. "This is the second test I did. That black line rising there, that's promising." He tapped some more on the keyboard. "These results are a strong indication that she will likely be coming out of the coma soon." He took a step away so Sasha could get a closer look.

"Thank you," said Sasha. "For showing me that." She concentrated, trying to remember all the steps he had taken the time to point out to her.

Dr. Wagner shut down the machine. "I will be back tonight to check on her. If anything occurs in the meantime, you can get in touch with me."

Just then Dr. Cesero walked into the room. "Nurse Farkas can consult with me. I'll confer with you," he said. "We'll see you tonight, Dr. Wagner."

Dr. Wagner removed his white coat and set it on a chair, then laid the stethoscope on top of it. His eyes lifted, and he held Sasha's gaze for a moment, then gave her a quick smile and left the room.

It was late afternoon when the woman awoke. Sasha had been checking her vitals and stopped when her eyes fluttered open and appeared to focus on her.

"You're okay," Sasha said. "You're in a medical center. Can you speak?"

The woman's eyes darted around, taking in the room, then she looked back at Sasha. She tried to sit up at first but stayed where she was. Her voice came out raspy, barely above a whisper when she asked, "Can I get some water?"

Sasha reached into the small refrigerator beneath the sink for a cup of ice chards from the freezer and scooped some into a spoon. She brought it to the woman's mouth, who tentatively took a small piece.

"More?" asked Sasha.

The woman nodded, so Sasha fed her several more mouthfuls, then set down the cup. "I need to alert the doctor that you're awake." She started to turn when the woman surprised Sasha by grabbing her arm.

"What is it?" asked Sasha.

The woman glanced at the door, then back at Sasha's face and said in a low voice, "He hurts me."

"Who?" said Sasha, alarmed. "The doctor?"

"No." The woman lifted her head slightly, then licked her lips. "Don't tell them I told you." Her eyes pleaded with Sasha.

Sasha thought about her next words carefully. "If there is something you want to tell me, I can tell the doctor." She waited. The woman let go of Sasha's arm and leaned back on the pillow, appearing defeated.

The door flung open then and Dr. Cesero entered. "The patient is awake? When were you going to tell me this, Nurse Farkas?" The muscle in his jaw clinched several times.

"It just occurred, Dr. Cesero. I was about to get you when she asked for some ice chips."

He smiled down at the woman. "Nice to see you awake, Madeline. You gave everyone quite a scare. Can you tell me the month, dear?"

The woman's expression remained wary, but she slowly nodded and replied, "It's August."

"Do you remember what happened to you?" he asked.

The woman's face filled with fear. Dr. Cesero patted her on the arm. "You're going to be okay," he assured her. "Just rest. I'll let your husband know you're awake." She started to grab hold of his sleeve, then seemed to change her mind. He patted her hand and smiled.

After he left, Sasha checked Madeline's blood pressure, noting it had risen substantially since Dr. Cesero's visit. Sasha recognized raw fear when she saw it.

The day that Sasha set off for America, she kissed her mother on the cheek and clasped her hands before leaving their apartment in Budapest. "I'm going to be fine, *Anya*. I promise," Sasha assured her. "I'll soon be using my nursing training."

Her mother tried to smile, but Sasha could see anxiety mapping her face. Sasha's heart clenched as she noticed how her mother had aged in the last few years, her hair shot through with streaks of silver where there had been none before. She memorized her mother's face, then buttoned her brown wool jacket and wrapped the scarf her mother had knitted last winter about her neck. "I must go," she said, giving her another long hug, then squeezing her hand one last time before leaving the apartment, suitcase in hand.

Sasha made her way through the familiar streets of her neighborhood and onto the main artery that led downtown. As she walked, her heart pounded in her chest. She felt very nervous, but also excited, and hopeful. She assured herself over and over that everything was going to be okay. It had to be. She knew she had met Andreas for a reason. Out of breath, she finally reached the coffee shop where he had told her to meet him.

When Sasha entered the coffeehouse, she saw Andreas leaning against the counter. He didn't smile or greet her and seemed different from the several times they'd met. He walked over and placed a hand on her back, shoving her toward the door.

"What's wrong?" she said as they left the coffeeshop.

"We need to go right now." He spoke in a harsh tone she didn't recognize. "We only have a few hours until the ship leaves."

"Ship?" said Sasha, stopping in the middle of the sidewalk. "I thought we were taking an airplane."

"Change of plans," he said as a van pulled up next to the curb. A tall, muscular man with tattooed arms got out of the driver's side and slid open the van door. Inside were several women. They stared at her, fearful confusion in their eyes.

Sasha backed up, then glanced around for an exit path. "I don't think I want to go any more," she said.

Andreas grabbed her arm and pushed her toward the van. "You've already taken your first loan. Unless you can give the money back right now with interest, you're getting in."

A boulder of fear lodged in her stomach, Sasha climbed into the van.

## 9

Just as Hans finished for the day, his phone buzzed. A text read, *Report to the clinic immediately.* How had they gotten his cellphone number? He could never have imagined being in a situation like this, his and his mother's lives threatened. A surge of helpless anger washed through him.

He wondered if the woman had taken a turn for the worst. He thought about changing into his street clothes but time seemed to be of the essence. As he rushed out the door, he passed Chuck on his way in, who gave Hans a startled look when he saw him in his scrubs. "Hey, is everything okay?" he called after Hans. "Did they bring in an emergency case?"

Hans kept walking, waving a hand in the air without turning around. Things are far from okay, he thought as he raced to his car.

Sasha rubbed the woman's pale hands to improve circulation. As she did so, Madeline remained silent, staring straight ahead with a blank expression on her face.

"Does that feel better?" Sasha asked as she moved to rub her feet.

The women nodded and continued gazing past Sasha. "Thank you," she said, her words emotionless.

While a part of Sasha wanted Madeline to confide in her about who hurt her, the other part told her to mind her own business. Not yet legal and still in debt for her passage here, Sasha was on thin ice, as they said in America. She certainly didn't need to cause trouble for herself. By the time she finished massaging Madeline's feet and washed her hands, Sasha had convinced herself that remaining quiet was the best plan of action. But when Madeline gripped the bedsheet in her hands at the sound of the door opening, Sasha's resolve to remain neutral wavered.

Sasha saw it was Dr. Wagner, and relief swept through her. The tension in his body seemed to loosen as their eyes met. "Nurse Farkas." He nodded to her. Then he looked at Madeline and exclaimed, "I see our star patient has awoken from her nap." He went to the side of the bed. "I'm Dr. Wagner, and you are?"

When the woman didn't say anything, Sasha answered for her. "Madeline."

"Madeline, how are you feeling?" he asked.

Madeline looked to Sasha and back to Dr. Wagner, her eyes cautious.

"Dr. Wagner is a neurologist," said Sasha, going to stand beside the bed. "He's here to help you."

"I have a terrible headache," she said finally, "and I feel dizzy."

"That's to be expected," said Dr. Wagner, who checked her pupils, then the paper chart. He nodded approvingly. "You are a lucky woman. I think you will be fine, but I'm going to do a test to make sure."

As he prepared to attach the EEG electrodes to her scalp, Madeline's eyes teared up. She opened her mouth to speak, but then shut it again.

"The test won't hurt," Dr. Wagner assured her just as Dr. Cesero walked in.

"How is she?" he asked as Antonio rolled a cart by in the hallway.

"From what I can tell, she is fine, but I'm going to run another test to confirm."

Dr. Cesero checked his watch. "Make it quick. Someone is coming to get her in thirty minutes."

Madeline closed her eyes and made a low whimpering sound.

After Cesero left the room, Hans noted that Madeline had become visibly upset. He put his hand on her shoulder. "Are you not feeling well?"

"I...I," the woman stammered, her eyes darting back and forth between Sasha and Hans.

Madeline didn't have a chance to finish her sentence because the redhead came storming in just then. "Dr. Wagner, please be expedient. Madeline needs to get back to her family. That way you can get back to yours," she said, emphasizing yours.

Hans wheeled the EEG machine close to the bed and began prepping Madeline. All he wanted at the mention of his mother was to finish what he was doing and call Mead-owbrook to make certain she hadn't been harmed.

Alina's comment about Dr. Wagner's family made Sasha question how such a seemingly nice man had gotten tangled up in all of this. Was Cesero threatening his family to make him treat Madeline? Sasha watched the doctor work. She suspected that he believed in, "First, do no harm." She remembered that ideal well and how she had dreamed about doing great nursing work and helping many people. The more Sasha considered the woman's anxious state of mind and her earlier outburst, the more she realized—this wasn't the first time a patient had come through this clinic who appeared fearful. There was more going on here than Sasha had been willing to face.

As the van made its way through the crowded streets of Budapest, Sasha eyed the door handle and calculated how long it would take her to unlock it and get out. She knew many of the streets would now be full of pedestrians. Could she escape quickly and get lost in the crowd? But then what? Where would she and her mother go? Andreas knew where they lived. She had also spent the money he'd given her for the trip to America on food and medication for her mother.

When the van stopped an hour later, Sasha knew they had arrived at the port, because she heard a ship's horn blow. She peered through the front window to see they were in a line of vehicles waiting to pass through an inspection station. As they edged toward the man directing the cars onto the dock, she struggled with the decision to run. But common sense told her the outcome. It would be suicide to make a getaway —even if she succeeded.

"Maybe we will have a nice cabin," said one girl as the scent of salty air and fish entered the van. She was very young, with wavy, fair hair.

The driver sniggered at her comment and said to Andreas, "She'll spend plenty of time in a nice cabin. On her back." The two had a good laugh as the meaning of what he said snaked tendrils of terror throughout Sasha's body.

## 10

Dr. Wagner appeared tense as he performed the EEG on Madeline. He looked as if he might ask the woman a question but remained silent. When the results were ready, he nodded as he reviewed them. His shoulders relaxed, and he moved his head from side to side to stretch his neck muscles.

After some time, Sasha broke the silence. "How does the EEG look, Dr. Wagner?"

"Very promising," he said. "All brain activity is back to normal." He turned to Madeline. "How is the headache now that we've given you some pain reliever?"

"Better, doctor, thank you."

Then he faced Sasha. "How long have you worked here?"

Sasha swallowed, then answered, "Three years."

Dr. Wagner glanced at the door, then into Sasha's eyes. He said in a low voice, "She is well physically, but I'm not sure about emotionally. I suspect the overdose was a suicide attempt. She really needs to be checked out by a mental health professional."

Sasha liked the doctor and felt she should somehow warn him. She took a deep breath and replied, "I think it's best for you and your family that you stick to her physical state when speaking to Dr. Cesero."

He frowned and asked, "Are you speaking from personal experience?"

Sasha was struggling to form an answer when Dr. Cesero walked in and asked, "Is Madeline ready to leave, Dr. Wagner?"

The doctor turned away from Sasha and straightened up. "Yes, her test results came out fine." He glanced at Madeline, who turned her head away and held the blanket tight against her chest.

"Very well, your services are no longer needed," said Dr. Cesero. "You can see your way out now."

Then he turned to Sasha and snapped, "Nurse Farkas, help Madeline get ready to go. Make it snappy. We have an abdominoplasty waiting in room one."

When Cesero dismissed Hans, he felt relief sweep through him. As he left the room, he tried to catch the nurse's gaze, but she was already prepping Madeline. Hans thought of Cesero's repeated warning about his family. His first stop would be Meadowbrook Village to make sure his mother was okay.

Sasha couldn't help feeling disappointed when Dr. Wagner left. A part of her even felt envious as he rushed out of the room. She imagined him hurrying to his wife, who was probably beautiful, like the women who ate lunch at the nearby restaurant where Dr. Cesero would send her to pick up takeout for him. While she waited, she'd sneak glances at the women as they ate their salads and sipped wine, their faces made up perfectly and their long, elegant legs showing beneath flowing skirts and dresses. Sometimes, Sasha imagined herself as one of them. What would it feel like, she wondered, to have her life to herself?

When they passed through inspection at the dock, Sasha hoped the authorities would check inside the van. Instead, she saw the driver slip one of the officers a wad of cash. The man then quickly waved them through. She took a good look at her companions in the van. Besides the young girl, there was a stocky, older woman, and a striking young woman about Sasha's age in her late twenties with curly, raven hair and large brown eyes. She was much more buxom than Sasha could ever hope to be, and the driver kept glancing back and leering at her. Sasha felt like giving her something to cover up her bosom but decided to mind her own self.

When the driver stopped the van, Andreas got out and pulled the door open. He grabbed Sasha's arm tightly and yanked her out of the van, then said in her ear, "Do as you're told, and you'll get to America in one piece." Then he pushed her toward a tall woman with red hair waiting by the dock in front of a large ship. Sasha looked around and prayed for help. She had made a terrible mistake, and now it was too late.

Hans pulled into Meadowbrook Village and parked the car, then sat for a moment and steadied himself. The sun was low in the evening sky, the air still warm. Once he felt calm enough to go in, he got out of the car and locked it, then glanced around the parking lot. This whole experience had made him paranoid.

"I'm making a surprise visit to my mother," he told the woman at the front desk. "Can you tell me where she is right now?"

"Of course, Mrs. Wagner is in the entertainment room watching her favorite show."

Hans smiled and headed down the hall. When he saw his mother sitting in her wheelchair in front of the television, he felt immense relief. He waited in the doorway until a commercial came on, then approached her.

"Hans! What a nice surprise. This isn't your day to visit." She studied his face. "Is something wrong?"

Hans shook his head. "No, I was just in the area, and I thought I'd stop in and see how you're doing."

His mother's round face lit up. "I'm doing very well. Would you like to get a cup of cocoa with me?"

"What about your show?" He leaned down and straightened the rose-colored afghan she kept across her lap, even in summertime.

His mother waved her hand at the television, then turned

her wheelchair toward the doorway. "I'd much rather talk to you."

Hans walked behind the chair and wheeled his mother out of the room, heading to the dining hall. "Have you been good like you promised me and are going to physical therapy?" he asked.

"Yes, and the therapist thinks I may be able to walk some before long. Probably not to the dining hall, but around my room at least. I can't tell you how terrible it's been to be a prisoner in this chair since I broke my hip."

At the mention of the word prisoner, Hans thought of the clinic, and the nurse's face flashed before him. Cesero and the redhead didn't have any compunction about threatening Hans to treat Madeline. Was it possible that they had something on Sasha? She couldn't be there against her will, could she?

## 11

The man who had dropped off Madeline the other night came to retrieve her. As he escorted her into the elevator, the young woman kept her head down, her shoulders slouched forward. When she turned around, she glanced up suddenly and met Sasha's eyes before the elevator door slid shut. Sasha recognized that resigned look all too well.

The redhead, dressed in tailored gray pants and a short red jacket, marched Sasha and the other women down the dock toward the ship. The captain stood welcoming guests onboard. When they were next in line, the woman turned to them, a warning glare in her eyes. "Smile, or the other passengers will think you aren't here of your own accord. You did decide to travel with us all by yourselves, didn't you ladies?" Then she turned and greeted the captain, who was older, with white hair and leathery skin.

"Alina, you're back," he said, shaking her hand.

"There's four this time," she told him. "The older one will work in the kitchen." Disinterest showed on her face as she stood erect, her body in a state of self-restraint.

The captain's eyes roamed over all of them. "One of them has nursing skills?" he asked.

"Yes, that one," said Alina, pointing to Sasha.

"Not bad to look at, either," he commented, then motioned for them all to climb aboard.

Alina took them below deck and led them along a narrow passageway until they came to a room with a metal door. She held out her hand and shouted over the rumble of the ship's engine. "Give me your passports for safekeeping."

Sasha's heart sank as she pulled her purse tight against her chest while the other women mumbled amongst themselves.

"I'm not going to argue this point." Anger colored Alina's cheeks.

The other women gave her their passports, and Sasha reluctantly followed suit.

Once she had their documentation in hand, Alina unlocked the door and ordered Sasha and the two younger women to enter the cramped room, which had an unpleasant damp, musty smell. As she began to pull the door shut, the fair-haired girl said, "But there are only two beds in here."

Alina stiffened, and her eyes hardened. "Be glad you have beds," she said, the harsh tone of her voice a reality check for Sasha that the three of them only had one another to count on. "I want to see all of you ready for dinner when I come back in an hour. You better have bought nice dresses with the money Andreas gave you, as instructed."

She slammed the small door and locked it from the

outside just as the ship's horn blew, signaling they would soon be leaving the port and the only home Sasha had ever known. As the realization that she'd lost complete control over her life settled in, Sasha wrapped her arms around herself and held back tears.

On the way out of his mother's care facility, Hans thought how there were times he worried she might never leave Meadowbrook. He wanted her to come home, feed the birds, watch her TV shows and chat on the phone with her friends. But she seemed to be doing well here, and from a physical perspective, this was the best place for her right now.

Hans stopped by the reception desk before heading out the door. The nurse on duty set down a cup of coffee. "Yes, Dr. Wagner. Can I help you with something?"

"I know you have my cellphone number in case of emergencies, but I also have a pager number I'd like to give you as a backup."

In his car a couple minutes later, Hans leaned his head back on the seat. Now that the adrenaline had ebbed, he realized how truly tired he was. He'd go straight home and shower and get some rest. He finally had to admit to himself he had been worried, both for himself and his mother. He had never felt physically threatened before, and Cesero and the redhead involving his mother made him shudder. He hoped it was all behind them now.

"Good job today, Nurse Farkas," said Dr. Cesero, surprising Sasha. He was rarely one to give compliments. An hour earlier, they had finished a 4-hour abdominoplasty and liposuction. She had just completed her post-op work of getting the patient comfortable and administering pain reliever. Though she missed home and her mother, and it seemed to be taking forever to save enough money to pay off her passage here, Sasha was grateful for the surgical skills she had acquired these last three years.

"We have a rhinoplasty early tomorrow morning. Why don't you leave for the day? I can monitor the patient."

"Okay, thank you, Dr. Cesero," said Sasha, delighted to be leaving midday. "What time do you need me in the morning?"

"Five a.m. sharp." He began to tap something into his phone.

Sasha nodded, then headed to get her things. Once in her car, she checked the time on the dashboard. If she hurried, she could get home in time to call her mother before she went to bed.

When Sasha arrived home a few minutes later, she rang her mother's number and waited. The cost to use her cell-phone to call Hungary was very expensive, but they had agreed to not talk long or very often. Just a brief hello to let each know they were okay.

Finally, her mother answered. "Sasha, is that you?"

"Yes, *Anya*, it's me. The doctor gave me the afternoon off, so I'm calling you."

"The afternoon off. You must be doing a good job."

Sasha smiled. "The doctor did say that today. How are you feeling?"

"The medicine is helping me breathe. Thank you for the money."

"We can't talk long, but I wanted to hear your voice and make sure you are well," said Sasha.

"I am. Except for wishing to see you in person, all is well."

Sasha took a sip of water, willing the lump of emotion forming in her throat down. It seemed like forever since she'd held her mother's hands.

"Are you there, Sasha?"

"I'm here, *Anya*. Forgive me. I had a long day."

"Such an important job you have," said her mother. "I don't have much news for you, but I do have a favor to ask. For my friend Natalya. I told you her daughter, Anna, had gone to America and no one has heard from her."

"I remember," said Sasha.

"Anna phoned Natalya last week. She said she was in California, where you are, but then the call was lost."

"What do you want me to do?"

"Can you look for her? Ask around? I can mail you a photo of her, so you know what she looks like."

"I can try."

"I told Natalya that if anyone could help, it would be my Sasha."

When Sasha hung up, she sighed, thinking how she'd have to tell her mother yet another lie. She couldn't possibly start sniffing around when her own situation was on such unsteady ground. She'd managed for the last three years to keep moving forward without making any waves that might threaten getting her immigration papers. Sasha wasn't willing to jeopardize that.

## 12

Hans woke up in the early morning before his alarm sounded and turned it off. Then he lay his head back on the pillow and listened to the silence in his condo. Usually, he enjoyed collecting his thoughts in the quiet time before preparing for a shift, but this morning the hush felt like it was closing in around him. He was reminded of the events at Cesero's medical center. In normal circumstances, he would report what he'd seen to the medical board, but these were far from normal circumstances. He heaved himself out of bed to get ready.

After showering and dressing, Hans made himself a cup of strong coffee and an omelet and sat down at the kitchen table. He opened his laptop and scanned the headlines, then typed the address of the medical clinic into the search bar. A website popped up. There was Dr. Cesero and all the usual marketing information about the wonders of plastic surgery. Hans clicked to the "About Us" page to find Cesero pictured with a team of nurses. None of them were the nurse he'd worked with. There were also no photos of the redhead.

Sasha parked her Honda in the medical center lot a few minutes before five a.m. and gathered her things. She liked to be a little early to have a chance to get settled. The elevator door opened on the medical center floor, and she walked past reception and started down the hallway when she heard a moan. Her heart rate hitching up several notches, she stole down the hall and peeked around the corner. There on the floor was Dr. Cesero clutching his stomach. Sasha threw down her things and hurried over to him. She knelt next to him, noting a knife protruding from his abdomen. "I'll call an ambulance," she said.

"No ambulance. You need to take care of me," he gasped, his face red and sweaty.

"But what if the knife hit an artery or you have internal injuries?" she said, surveying the blood creeping out from around the blade and onto his shirt. "I'm not a doctor."

"Call Dr. Wagner," he said.

"I don't have his number."

"I have it." Dr. Cesero groaned as he reached into his jacket pocket and removed his phone. Then he caught his breath before tapping in a code and pressing a number and handing it to her. Sasha took the cell and listened as it went to voicemail.

"This is Dr. Hans Wagner. Leave a message after the tone. If this is a life-threatening emergency, please hang up and immediately dial 9-1-1."

Sasha kept her eye on Dr. Cesero as she spoke into the phone, trying to refrain from sounding panicked. "Hi, Dr. Wagner, this is Nurse Farkas at Dr. Cesero's office. He has had a serious accident. Could you come here as soon as possible?" She hung up and set the phone down on the cool tile, then checked out the wound.

"If I take out the knife, you'll bleed out," she said, stating the obvious. When she realized they might not be alone, she surveyed the long hallway, then checked behind her. "Is there anyone else here?"

"The man who stabbed me left," Dr. Cesero said. "Lock the front door."

Sasha hurried to the front and locked it. Then she grabbed a pillow from a surgical room and used it to elevate Dr. Cesero's head. Just as she tried to think what to do next, his cellphone lit up. The display read: *Dr. Wagner.* She grabbed the phone and pressed answer, putting it up to her ear. "Dr. Wagner, Nurse Farkas."

"Is everything okay?"

"Actually, it's not. Dr. Cesero has been stabbed. The knife is still in him. He's stable for now."

"I'll be right there. I'm close by at the hospital. Hold tight."

Sasha hung up the phone, her chest filling with relief at having reached him. Dr. Cesero couldn't die. He was her lifeline here in America.

Hans was intubating a patient in emergency with a head and chest injury from a car accident when he felt his phone vibrate in his pocket. He immediately thought of his mother, then reminded himself he had also given the care facility his pager number. He had to get the man breathing so he could assess the damage to his skull. When he finished with the intubation and the patient was receiving sufficient air, he examined the man's head. A severe cut in the occipital region but no visible fractures.

The hospital's thoracic surgeon arrived then, slightly out of breath. "I'm glad you were available," he said to Hans. "I just got out of surgery. Thanks for the intubation. How's the rest of him?"

"A deep gash in his occipital region. We'll see what the MRI picks up," said Hans. He pulled his phone out of his pocket. There was a voicemail from the medical center.

"I can take over if you're needed elsewhere," said the surgeon. "I'll want your input once the MRI results come in. He's going to need surgery on his chest stat."

Hans nodded and walked away to check his messages. He waited to hear Cesero's voice and was surprised when the nurse began speaking.

"I need to go out for a while," he told the head nurse at the critical care desk. "An emergency with my mother. Dr. Everson is with the car accident patient. Let him know I had to leave. I will try and be back soon."

Then he grabbed his bag from the locker room and sped out the door. Cesero getting stabbed concerned him, but he worried even more about the nurse's safety.

While she waited anxiously for Hans, Sasha examined the blood loss from the knife wound. It had slowed, which was good. She took Dr. Cesero's wrist in her hands and checked his pulse. It had become thready. He was sweating profusely and, she could tell, in great pain. She thought about asking him who had done this, but she was afraid of knowing the answer and what she would do with the information.

Sasha didn't have any money left over after ensuring her mother was well-stocked to buy a fancy dress before leaving America. As she stared at the meager contents of her suitcase that night before dinner on the ship, she had no idea what she would wear. She feared the fury of Alina, who was seemingly in charge of them. Then the fair-haired girl pulled a dress out of her bag and handed it to Sasha.

"What about you?" Sasha asked her.

"I have two," she said. "That will look good on you."

"I'll pay you back when we get to America. What is your name?"

The girl smiled. "Annalise."

Sasha looked to the other woman, who had packed herself into a tight black dress. "I am Sonja," she said.

Keys sounded, and Alina slapped the door open. After surveying all three of them with a critical eye, she marched over to Sonja and tousled her black, curly mane of hair.

"You two are going to eat at the captain's table," she said to Sasha and Annalise. Then she yanked the front of Sonja's dress lower to expose more of her ample bosom. "I have other plans for you."

## 13

When Hans got to the medical center doors, he rapped hard several times. The nurse answered. She had blood on her hands.

"Where is he?"

"In the hallway."

She locked the door behind him, then they made their way to Cesero. He was lying on the floor, barely conscious, his head elevated on a pillow. Hans crouched beside him.

"Do you think the knife hit the femoral artery?" she asked.

"I can't be sure until we get it out. While I'd like to treat him in a room, moving him could jar the knife and have fatal consequences. I'll need to take it out here." He removed the needle and coagulant from his bag and prepared them, then injected the solution into Cesero's arm. "Can you get some towels? I may need to cauterize his blood vessels."

When Nurse Farkas returned with the towels, he gripped the knife and said, "Be ready to apply pressure. Hopefully, the coagulant will stop the bleeding, and I can get him stitched up." Hans pulled the knife up and out as Cesero screamed. The nurse quickly applied the towels, and Hans was relieved when they didn't immediately become soaked with blood. After a few moments, he lifted them to survey the wound.

"It looks like his femoral was spared," he said, then rested back on his heels and gently placed his hand on her arm. "What is your name?"

"Farkas."

"I mean your first name."

She appeared hesitant about answering him. "It's Sasha," she said softly.

"Please, call me Hans." He smiled, then removed his hand from her arm. "I'm going to need antiseptic and supplies for stitching him up, then we can move him to a bed. Thank you for the care you gave him."

As Sasha watched Hans work on Dr. Cesero, she admired how he remained calm. He talked in a steady voice and worked quickly, but methodically. Once he finished stitching the wound, the two of them hoisted Dr. Cesero up and got him into a bed. While Hans washed up, Sasha started Dr. Cesero on an IV drip and gave him pain medication.

"Thank you so much for coming," she said. "I'm sorry we had to call on you again."

Hans glanced at the patient, who had dozed off. "Can I speak to you out of the room?" he asked her.

When they were in the hallway, Sasha noted the blood on the floor. She would have to clean that before it stained.

"What happened before I came?" Hans waited as she debated how to describe the whole terrifying situation.

She finally pulled her gaze from the blood stain and looked into his face. "We were supposed to do a rhinoplasty at six this morning, so he had me come in at five. I found him like this when I got here."

"Was there anyone else present?"

Sasha shook her head.

"We need to call the police." He pulled his phone from his pocket.

"No, you can't," said Sasha. "I'm sorry. I know this puts you in a bad position. When Dr. Cesero comes to, I'll tell him I stitched him up. That way he won't know you were here." She held her breath as she waited to see what Hans would say.

His expression was one of concern. "I don't know how you're involved in all of this, Sasha, but I don't think you're safe here."

"Nothing like this has ever happened before." She tried to keep an even tone in her voice. "I'm sure there is a good explanation."

Hans raised his eyebrows. "There is never a good explanation for attempted murder." His phone buzzed just then and he checked the screen, his brow furrowing. "I need to get back to the hospital. Give me your phone, and I'll type in my contact."

Sasha pulled her cell out of her pocket and gave it to him. Hans punched in his number and handed it back to her. "Please call me if you need anything. And let me know how he is doing."

"I will."

After Hans left, Sasha locked the door again, then stood in the waiting room for a moment, steadying herself. The enormity of the last hour finally hit her. Hans was right. Things were terribly out of hand. When she finally felt steady enough, she went to check on Dr. Cesero. Then she got to work removing the blood from the floor.

Hans got back to the hospital in time to check on the accident victim and advise before Everson took him into surgery. Then he went into his office and shut the door. He sat at his desk, staring at his phone, then looked up a number. His college buddy, Robert, worked for British Intelligence and was the only person Hans could think of to call for this brand of advice. He dialed his number using the hospital phone.

Robert answered on the second ring. "Is that you, Hans?"

"Hope I'm not catching you at a bad moment. I've got a situation on my hands."

Robert chuckled. "That's a first. It's usually me calling you."

Hans smiled, recalling the last time his friend had been in town and needed emergency medical assistance. "I think we can safely say that you owe me."

"I'm listening," said Robert.

"There's a plastic surgeon, a Nathaniel Cesero, who seems to be involved with a rough crowd. I just got back from stitching him up after a stab wound." After he said this out loud, Hans realized just how bad the situation was.

"How did you end up at his office?" asked Robert.

"There is this woman. A redhead. I don't know her name. But she and the doctor threatened my mother, so I was forced to assist with a patient. An overdose. And now the stabbing. There's also a nurse. Sasha Farkas. I'm not sure how she fits in, but I fear she's being coerced."

After a couple of beats, Robert said, "My advice. Stay as far away from that as possible. It sounds like organized crime. Could be Russian. You don't want to get mixed up in that. Everyone is fair game. Including your mother."

Hans knew Robert was right, but he kept picturing Sasha's face and the fear that swept across it when he mentioned going to the police. "I don't think I can leave it alone."

Robert sighed. "Of course, you can't. You nearly got us kicked out of the dorm at Harvard with that stray cat you took in. Let me make some calls about Sasha, Cesero, and the center. I'll need the address."

"Thank you, old friend," said Hans.

"Don't thank me yet. And please, watch your back. Do you still have the beretta I showed you how to shoot?"

"In my safe at home."

"Dust it off, and don't hesitate to use it."

## 14

As Sasha finished cleaning up the blood, she suddenly remembered the abdominoplasty patient. With all that was going on with Dr. Cesero, she nearly forgot about her! She ran to her room and threw open the door, then gasped at what she saw. The bed was empty, and the sheets were stained with blood. Sasha had managed to keep herself together until now, but this had her trembling uncontrollably. She hugged her arms and took deep gulping breaths to quell the panic racing through her.

Sasha left the room and went to check on Dr. Cesero. If he was awake, she could ask him about the patient. He was still asleep but mumbling something. She approached quietly and came to stand next to him, straining to hear his words. At first it was bits and pieces of another language, then he said something that surprised her, "*Ostanavlivat'sya.*" Russian for stop. This was the first time she'd heard Dr. Cesero speak anything but English or Spanish.

Shocked to hear him speaking Russian, Sasha realized how little she knew about her employer. Driven by a desire to find out what was really going on here, she carefully slid her hand into his right pocket and fished out the key chain he always carried. She left the room and went a few doors down the hall. At his office door, she let herself in and gently closed the door, then turned the lights on. Sitting on the plush leather chair at his desk, she pulled open the top drawer. Nothing but paperclips and rubber bands and some chewing gum. The next drawer she tried to open was locked. She checked the keys on the ring, locating a small one that looked like it would fit and put it in the lock and turned. The drawer slid open, and she gasped. Dozens of passports. With shaking fingers, she picked them up one by one and opened them. All women her age or younger. Then she came to her passport. Dr. Cesero had told her the authorities were holding onto it while they processed her green card. Just then she heard something in the hallway, and her heart jumped into her mouth.

There was a rapping on the door, and Alina's voice called out, "Nathaniel, are you in there? What was the SOS call about?"

Sasha closed the desk drawer as quietly as possible, then glanced around for some place to hide. She was about to climb under his desk when she heard Alina retreat. Racing across the room, she waited for a moment at the door, listening, then quietly opened it and stepped into the hallway, shutting the door with a soft click behind her. After she dropped Dr. Cesero's keys into her pocket, she made her way toward the room where he lay unconscious. She heard Alina exclaim, "Oh, my god, Nathaniel!"

When Sasha walked in, Alina spun around with an accusing look on her face. "What in the hell happened to him? And why aren't you helping him?"

"I had to get more gauze pads," said Sasha, pulling a handful out of her pocket. "I don't know what happened to him. I got here at five a.m., as he told me to, and he was lying on the floor with a knife in him. I administered some antico-agulant and removed the knife and stitched him up."

"And you're sure you did a good job?" Alina looked doubtful.

"Of course. I also gave him pain reliever and antibiotics. But there is another problem."

Alina threw up her hands, then slapped them down on her black leather skirt. "What more could there be?"

"The abdominoplasty patient we worked on yesterday is gone."

In the three years Sasha had known Alina, she had never seen her look frightened until now. The woman's eyes widened, and her face turned white. After a few tense moments, she finally asked, "When is he going to wake up? I need to find out what happened to that patient."

Sasha checked his vitals, then calculated how long it had been since she'd given him the pain medicine. "He should be conscious in about an hour. He lost a lot of blood, so he'll be weak, but you should be able to talk to him."

Alina took a bottle out of her purse and shook a pill into her palm, then swallowed it. Sasha knew what it was.

It was nearly morning when Sonja came back to the cabin that first night on the ship. Pretending to be sleeping, Sasha opened her eyes a crack and watched as the girl took off her dress and put on her nightgown. She looked terrible, her face streaked with tears. When Sonja lay down, Sasha heard her wince, then begin to cry softly. What terrible mistake had the three of them made? How Sasha wished she was at home with her mother. Though her night dining with the captain appeared to be much better than Sonja's, who was to say what might happen next?

In the morning, Alina came into their room and went straight to Sonja's bed. She stood standing over her with her hands on her hips. "I heard you cried last night. I don't want that to happen ever again. Be grateful you're going to America."

"He hurt me," said Sonja.

Alina reached into her pocket and pulled out a pill that she handed to Sonja. "For pain and to forget," she told her. Then she turned her attention to Sasha. "Get dressed. I have a job for you."

Hans finished his shift and checked his phone for the tenth time in the last couple of hours. Nothing from Sasha. The more he thought about it, the more certain he felt that she was in danger. He decided to go check on things.

When Hans arrived at the building and went up to Cesero's floor, he tried knocking on the door, but no one answered. Frustrated, he decided to go back to his car and wait. He should have insisted Sasha give him her phone number. He strummed his fingers on the steering wheel. Now what? He had to be back at the hospital in twelve hours. He should go home and sleep but he couldn't leave without knowing Sasha was safe.

## 15

Sasha walked out of the medical center in the early evening with what looked like a wad of bedding in her arms. Hans watched as she hurried to a battered Honda and opened the trunk, then threw the armful inside. He got out of his car and headed toward her. When he was a few feet away, she spun around and put her hands to her chest.

"I'm sorry to have frightened you," he apologized as he came to stand in front of her.

It took her a moment to regain her bearings. "Doctor, I mean, Hans, what are you doing here?"

Hans looked at the bedding, which was covered in blood, then met her eyes. "Is Cesero okay?"

"Yes, he's stable." She closed the trunk of her car. "Those are from a surgery this morning. I'm going to bring them home and wash them."

"Don't they have washing facilities here?"

"Yes...." Sasha's usually stoic expression softened then and tears threatened her beautiful brown eyes. He thought about reaching out to comfort her but he didn't want to overstep. Instead, he waited.

"Please forgive me," she said. "It's been a long day."

"Clearly," said Hans. "Tell me what happened."

Sasha glanced at the building and back at Hans. "You're a very nice man. You shouldn't be here."

"But I am," he said, holding her gaze.

How comforting it felt to have someone care about her, thought Sasha. But Hans was putting himself in danger being here. If Alina saw him, she would pull him back into her harrowing web, and Sasha didn't want that for him.

"I appreciate you checking on me, but it's best if you go home to your family," she said.

"My family is my mother," he replied. "And she's at her assisted living facility. I'm here to help you."

"I'm fine," she said. As dire as things were, somewhere in the back of her mind it registered that Hans wasn't married.

"I don't think you are fine. Are you off work?"

Sasha shook her head. "No, I need to go back in."

"Let me go in with you. I can check on Cesero."

"Alina is with him."

"Who is that?"

"The redhead who forced you to come here."

Hans looked at his watch. "I have to report to the hospital by midnight. If you get off sooner, text me. Either way, let me know what's going on."

Sasha felt relieved when Hans decided not to go into the building to check on Dr. Cesero. It was best he stayed away from Alina. Just being in her presence could only bring him trouble, and it seemed Hans knew that.

"Thank you again. I'll be okay," she said. Then she turned and headed back to the building. When she pulled open the heavy glass door, she resisted the urge to look back. Right now, she had bigger things to think about. Like how to slip Dr. Cesero's key back into his pocket undetected.

Standing in the hallway outside of his room five minutes later, Sasha shored up her shoulders and reminded herself that she had gotten through much worse than this. She walked into Dr. Cesero's room to see that he was still sleeping. Alina sat by his bed.

"Did you get rid of the sheets?" she asked Sasha.

"They're in my trunk. I'll take them to my apartment."

Alina turned away then, as if done with Sasha's mere presence. It was always this way with the woman. Some might say that trouble followed her, but Sasha knew the truth. Alina *was* the trouble, and Sasha stayed extremely wary around her. All Alina touched got scorched. Sasha counted herself among the lucky ones. At least so far.

When Alina told Sasha to get dressed that morning on the ship, she felt her stomach do uncomfortable flips.

"Now. We have an emergency," she ordered her.

Sasha got out of bed and scurried to her suitcase, then turned to Alina. "What should I wear?"

"Your regular clothes. Just hurry."

Sasha slipped on a pair of pants and a blouse, then followed Alina up to the deck. There they passed passengers lounging about, sipping drinks and eating breakfast in the early morning sun.

Alina walked quickly, taking long strides, and Sasha hurried to keep up. After passing several doors, they came to one that read Ship's Doctor. Alina put her hand on the doorknob and gave Sasha a warning look. "You better be as good a nurse as you claim to be."

In the doctor's office, a pregnant girl lay on a bed, her face covered in sweat. The doctor had his hands on her belly. When they walked in, he turned to them. "This is the nurse? Does she speak English?"

"Her English is very good, as are her nursing skills," Alina assured him.

The man handed Sasha a pair of scrubs. "Put these on and wash up. We're delivering a baby."

Sasha was in the bathroom when footsteps passed by in the medical center hallway. She heard men's voices speaking Russian, Alina talking to them. Pressing her ear against the door, she strained to hear what was being said. Her Russian was only fair. Her mother had always pushed her to learn English, instead. Sasha opened the bathroom door a crack and peeked out. At the end of the hallway, a muscular man held Alina by the arms and another man towered over her. He had switched to English now and was accusing her of reneging on their contract, while Alina swore that wasn't the case. To Sasha's horror, the man who had been yelling at Alina went into Dr. Cesero's room and a gunshot rang out.

Alina screamed after the shot fired. She tried to claw her way out of the man's grasp, but he held her tight.

The gunman came out of the room and said, "Take her to the car. I'll make sure no one else is here."

## 16

Her heart beating so fast she thought it might explode, Sasha glanced around the bathroom for a place to hide. Besides the stall, there was a narrow broom closet. She quickly pulled out the mop and broom and propped them in the corner, then squeezed inside and shut the door.

Some time passed. She began thinking the man might skip the bathroom when the door opened. Sasha held her breath. If there was a god, she prayed he would spare her mother the agony of never knowing what happened to her daughter. She heard the stall door open and slam against the wall, then boots stomped by the broom closet, and he left the room.

Sasha stayed in the closet for a long time, waiting to ensure they had left. When she finally got out, she turned on the faucet and splashed her face. After opening the bathroom door and peeking out, she walked down the quiet hallway. When she got to the room where Dr. Cesero was likely lying dead, she steeled herself, then pushed the door open. The man had shot him through the heart. The blood had soaked the front of his shirt. But the worst part was the look of shock on his face.

For a time, Sasha just stood there, staring. Then she shut the door and made her way to the break-room, where she gathered her things. When she got to Dr. Cesero's office and found the door kicked in, her heart jumped into her throat. Had they found the passports? She rushed to his desk and breathed a sigh of relief to see that it was still locked. Slipping the key in, she turned it, then opened the drawer. She grabbed her passport before leaving the office and hurrying to her car. Her hands shook as she steered the car out of the lot, hoping no one was watching her. She'd go home and lock herself in her apartment and figure out what to do next.

Hans arrived at the hospital at midnight and halfheartedly began making his rounds. Though he tried to push the vision of Sasha holding back tears out of his mind, he couldn't stop thinking about her. Now that he was here at the hospital, he was upset with himself for leaving her. True, she'd insisted she didn't want or need his help, but he was convinced her life was in danger, and that greatly troubled him. By the time he finished with his second patient, he had decided. Sasha needed his help, and Hans was going to insist that she let him help her.

When Sasha arrived in front of her apartment complex, she glanced up and spotted the gunman she'd seen at the medical center walking down the stairs. Eyes forward, she kept driving, slowly, her heart beating fast. She made a loop through the lot and went back out to the street. Sasha had no idea where she was going. She just knew her life depended on getting away.

At the stoplight, she glanced in her rearview mirror to make sure no one followed. Then she turned west and drove past the strip malls now quiet for the night, no cars in the lots, until she came upon a nightclub, the parking lot packed with cars. Maybe that would give her an opportunity to blend in until she figured out what to do next. She found a spot toward the back of the lot and turned off the engine. Loud music came from the building, and there were people smoking cigarettes outside. She'd be safe until the bar closed, but then what? She had nowhere to go.

She pulled out her cellphone and found Hans's number. After staring at it for a moment, she dialed and put the phone to her ear. Expecting to leave a message, she was surprised when he picked up.

"Sasha?"

"Yes, it's me."

"You don't sound good."

"Something else happened."

"Wait," he said, his tone sounding urgent. "I'll call you back in a minute."

Sasha hung up. He was probably in the middle of dealing with a patient. She should have thought of that. But when the minutes turned into a half hour, her heart sank. She wouldn't blame him for rethinking his offer to help, but now she felt more alone than ever.

"Sasha, I want to see you after class," said her schoolmaster. It was the beginning of the school year, and she was in arithmetic class. It was important she do well, so she could get into university. She hadn't had this teacher before, so she wasn't sure what he wanted with her.

When all the other students filed out of the room, she went to stand in front of his desk. He was a thin man with a balding head and wire rim glasses that perched partway down the straight slope of his nose. He shifted in his chair and cleared his throat before he spoke. "First, I would like to say I believe you have great promise. You are an excellent student. But it has come to my attention that you don't have appropriate clothing for the winter months soon to come."

Surprised at his concerns, Sasha felt her face heat up. While she struggled to think of how to respond, he continued, "If you aren't properly clothed, it will be difficult for you to learn your arithmetic." He leaned back in his chair and eyed her closely. "I have been an instructor for many years and have seen this before. Is your father employed?"

Sasha took a deep breath and looked down at her feet before raising her head and replying with a lie. "My father is dead."

The man's eyes filled with understanding. "And your mother?"

"She works as a seamstress, but there isn't always enough." Sasha could feel her face turning crimson with shame.

"Very well. Please do your best to at least get yourself

some boots. And perhaps your mother could line your old coat. That will be all." He went back to the papers on his desk as Sasha left the room.

## 17

Sasha laid her head back on the driver's seat and watched all the happy people coming and going from the bar. She wondered what it would be like to have such a seemingly carefree existence. She wasn't one for drinking, though. She had tried alcohol a few times and soon realized that being out of control was a poor choice for her. Remaining vigilant and alert had kept her safe. She checked her gas gauge. Nearly full, thank goodness. Then she closed her eyes to think through her next move. Instead, she found herself soon dozing off.

When Sasha awoke, she glanced around, disoriented. The parking lot was nearly deserted. She thought she saw a movement in the shadows and was about to turn the engine on when her phone buzzed. The display read Mercy General. She answered but didn't speak.

"Sasha? It's Hans. Are you there?"

Relief at hearing his voice flooding through her, Sasha answered, "Yes."

"I'm sorry I didn't call back sooner," he said. "An emergency with a toddler. What happened?"

"It's too much for the phone," she said. "Can I come to you?"

"Of course. How far away are you?"

Sasha calculated. "About ten minutes."

"I'll be waiting out front," Hans said.

When Sasha pulled into the hospital parking lot and saw Hans, she had to hold her breath to quell the urge to burst out crying. She rolled down her window, immensely grateful to see his smiling face.

"Park in the visitor section," he said. "We'll talk in my office."

Sasha parked, then they walked side by side into the hospital. When he opened his office door and invited her in, the feelings she'd been holding in swept through her, and she nearly sobbed. "Thank you. I had nowhere else to go."

Hans closed the door, then pulled out a chair for her to sit down. He sat himself across from her. "Tell me what happened." When she hesitated, he took her hands in his. They felt warm and reassuring.

"Earlier today, I discovered that the abdominoplasty patient was missing. Alina came in soon after and wanted to know what happened to Dr. Cesero and the patient. She had me put the sheets from the patient in my trunk, which is when you saw me. Then after I went back in, we had visitors. I was in the bathroom when they came, and I heard them shouting at her." She paused and swallowed. "While one man held Alina, the other went in and shot Dr. Cesero."

"Is he dead?" asked Hans.

"Yes. The man with the gun searched the rest of the office after he shot him."

"Sasha, how did you get out?" asked Hans as he scooted to the edge of his chair.

"I hid in the broom closet until they left. Then I tried to go home, but I saw one of the men in front of my apartment complex, so I left and called you."

After Sasha revealed how close she'd come to being killed, Hans felt the urge to pull her to him, but instead he held her hands more tightly. "Oh, Sasha, I'm so sorry you had to experience that. Did you know the men?"

"I know they're Russian."

"So, Robert was right."

"Who is Robert?"

"He's a good friend of mine with British Intelligence. We went to college together. He told me they were probably Russian mafia."

Sasha pulled her hands from his. "You told him about me?"

"I trust him with my life," Hans reassured her. He checked the time. "I'm off in a couple of hours. You'll be safe here, then we can go to my place."

Sasha gave a small nod of agreement, and Hans got up to leave.

"Do you happen to have some water?" she asked.

"I do." Hans pulled open a desk drawer and took out a water bottle and a bag of peanuts.

Sasha looked at the peanuts and water and then at Hans, an odd expression on her face. "Why are you helping me?"

Hans sensed that more than a casual answer was needed at that moment. "Because you appear to be a genuinely nice person. Though I've only known you for a short time, I can tell you are an excellent nurse. I'd like to help you get to a safe place where you can use those nursing skills."

Sasha smiled. "Thank you."

Hans gave her shoulder a squeeze, then left his office to check on the emergency room patients. He was concerned about the turn of events, but glad Sasha had come to him. When he'd answered her question about why he was helping her, he failed to tell Sasha his top reason. That since the moment he'd met her, she wasn't far from his mind.

When Hans left, Sasha opened the bottle of water and drank down half in one long gulp. She couldn't remember the last time she'd had a drink or something to eat. Then she opened the bag of peanuts and took a mouthful. As she chewed, she thought about Hans's comment about her being a nice person. He wouldn't have said that if he knew the things she had turned a blind eye to.

The delivery onboard the ship was a difficult one. The girl's cervix wouldn't dilate completely, but her water had broken, and she was crowning. The ship doctor gave her a local anesthetic and helped guide the baby out, but she tore badly. The doctor left Sasha to deal with her bleeding and the afterbirth while he cleaned up the baby and checked him.

When he finished, Alina came into the room and approached the doctor. Sasha was focused on cleaning up the mother but could hear what they were discussing. Alina asked if the baby was healthy and said she had a buyer in America. When the doctor assured her that all would go according to plan, Alina left.

The baby began crying then, and the doctor handed the infant to Sasha. "Have the mother feed him. I'll take over stitching her up."

When Sasha put the little boy in his mother's arms, she helped guide the infant to her breast. The girl gently kissed the top of the baby's head, joy on her face.

Sasha prayed that she was wrong about the baby's fate. But two weeks later when the ship docked in America, Alina held the bundled infant as they disembarked. Sasha watched as she brought the baby boy to a waiting couple. As the woman cooed and smiled at him, the man handed Alina a thick envelope. She slid it into her bag, then shook their hands, and they turned and walked away.

Her heart aching for the young mother, Sasha searched the crowd disembarking the ship, but she didn't see her. When Sasha met Alina's eyes, they narrowed. "Welcome to America," she said. "Keep your mouth shut, and one day you'll be an American citizen."

# 18

When Hans returned to his office, he found Sasha asleep in the recliner he used for naps in between patients. He gently closed his office door. She still wore her scrubs and had her purse on her lap, her hands grasping it. She must have sensed him looking at her, because suddenly she startled awake. At first, her eyes filled with confusion, then she recognized him.

"I'm sorry to wake you," he said. "I'm done with my shift. We can go."

Sasha sat up as he put out his hand. She glanced at it. "I can get up myself," she said.

Hans smiled. "I have no doubt of that." He kept his hand extended. "Think of this as practice."

"Practice?"

"Me helping you. I get the impression you aren't very good at accepting help."

Sasha took his hand, and he pulled her to her feet. That put them inches apart, and neither one of them moved. "I haven't had many people offer help," she said.

Enjoying being this close to Sasha and not wanting to break the spell, Hans didn't reply for a moment. "I am

84

offering you help, which is going to start with going to my house and getting some rest. Shall we?"

They decided it was best if Sasha followed Hans to his home, where she would park her car in his garage to get it out of sight. As she drove, she felt torn between curiosity about seeing where he lived and worry that she was making a mistake. She could be leading trouble straight to his door.

When they arrived at his condominium complex, the early morning sun was bright. Hans opened his garage door and waved her inside. Once her car was safely tucked away, they walked a path to his doorway lined with flowerbeds overflowing with red and white petunias. Inside, Sasha walked into a small living room brightly lit with floor to ceiling windows along one wall and an adjoining small kitchen. The living room held minimal furniture—a beige couch and armchair and a coffee table stacked with medical journals. Propped against the wall here and there were paintings consisting of brightly colored geometric shapes. When Hans noticed Sasha eyeing the artwork, he explained, "I moved in a few months ago and still haven't finished hanging things up."

"Your home is lovely," said Sasha, noting that the small hallway leading to back bedrooms had photos set along the floor. She walked over and picked one up. Hans at a younger age with an older man and woman standing in front of the ocean.

"That's my mother and father," he said.

She looked at Hans and back at the photo. "I can see the resemblance."

"My father passed away a few years ago," he said.

"No siblings?" she asked.

"None. How about you?"

"I'm an only child, too," she said, setting the picture back on the floor.

Hans suppressed a yawn with his hand. "I think we should get some sleep. I haven't gotten around to buying a bed for the guest room, but there's the couch."

"The couch will be perfect," she said.

As Sasha nestled into the sheets and blanket Hans gave her, she found herself quickly drifting off in sheer exhaustion.

When Sasha awoke, it was early afternoon. She had slept so soundly; she was still in the same position as when she fell asleep. After stretching the cricks out of the muscles in her neck, she got up and peered down the hallway. It was quiet, so Hans was probably still asleep. She went into the kitchen and pulled open the refrigerator to see it was well stocked. Then she checked a few cupboards and had an idea. After locating a large wooden cutting board, she got to work.

Hans awoke and stretched, then glanced at the clock to see it was nearly three. He had slept much longer than he'd anticipated. He pulled on some shorts and a T-shirt, then made his way to the front of the condo, where he found

Sasha in the kitchen, engrossed in cutting an apple. On the counter was his cutting board, piled high with olives, cucumbers, carrot sticks, cheese, and cold cuts. She began arranging the apple slices within the other food on the board.

"That looks delicious," he said, breaking her revery.

Sasha smiled for the first time since he'd met her. "I was afraid you might be upset that I made myself at home. I'm almost done."

Hans laughed. "Almost? That looks fit for an entire kingdom. What else does it need?"

Sasha held up a finger. "Do you have some crackers or small toasts?"

Hans opened the cupboard above her head and pulled down some wheat crackers. "Will these do?"

"Perfectly," said Sasha. She took a handful and fanned them out in a corner of the board.

"What would you like to drink?" he asked. "I have some wine and beer."

"A beer would be great," said Sasha, carrying the tray to the kitchen table.

Hans plunked two beers down and sat across from her. He picked up an olive.

"In Hungary, we call this a snacking tray," she said. "It needs no utensils or plates." Sasha took a cracker and piled it high with cold cuts and cheese and topped it off with a cucumber slice. "My favorite part is eating any combination I want. My mother and I used to have contests as to who could make the oddest combination of food."

Hans watched the happy glint in Sasha's eyes when she talked about her mother. As they ate, he also noticed her mannerisms had become less guarded. She seemed more relaxed than he'd seen her until now.

"Where in Hungary are you from?" he asked as he finished his beer.

"Budapest, all my life. The first time I left the city was to come here." When she mentioned coming to the States, anxiety crept into her tone.

"Another beer or something else to drink? I have bottled water." Hans asked. When she didn't answer, Hans got up and took two beers out of the fridge and opened them both. He set hers on the table and took a pull of his. Then he met her eyes. "In order for me to help you, I need you to tell me what's going on at Cesero's medical center."

Sasha picked up the fresh beer and tore at the edge of the label. She took a deep breath, her eyes filling with sadness.

"Take your time," said Hans.

Sasha wanted to tell Hans everything. He was being so kind. And he had come to her rescue. Certainly, she owed him the truth. But Sasha hesitated, realizing that her real reservations weren't about not trusting him. Sasha was afraid that if she told Hans the truth, he would think less of her. Then would he still feel she deserved his help?

# 19

"I'm not sure where to start," said Sasha.

"How about at the beginning."

Sasha took a sip of beer, then cradled the bottle in her hands. "My mother was young, just sixteen when she had me. The plan had been to put me up for adoption, but once she held me, she couldn't let me go." Sasha paused for a moment, aware she was telling Hans things she had never shared with anyone. "My mother raised me as best she could, but her health hasn't always been good. She became very ill after my birth. I suspect there was an infection that lingered. She also always put me first. She would give food to me rather than eat it herself."

"It sounds like she loves you very much," said Hans quietly.

Sasha swallowed the lump of emotion in her throat and nodded.

"What about your father?"

Sasha sighed. "For many years, my mother wouldn't tell me who he was. She would say it didn't matter. But when I began studying nursing and realized the importance of genetics, I talked her into telling me. She did with the promise that I would never approach him. He's married. A shipping merchant in Budapest, and from what I could tell, wealthy. While I didn't approach him, I did see where he works. I waited outside in my car. Then I followed him to his home and watched as he walked to the front door of an entirely different family."

As Hans listened to Sasha relay her story, he could only imagine how difficult the road had been for her and her mother. "Where did you get your nursing degree?" he asked.

"Semmelweis University."

"That school has a good reputation."

Sasha smiled. "I graduated at the top of my class."

"That doesn't surprise me," he said. "But how did you pay for the schooling?"

Sasha frowned. "I worked many odd jobs for two years, and I took out loans. I send money to my mother so she can pay them." She took a deep breath. "You are probably wondering how I ended up here."

"Tell me when you're ready," said Hans. He noticed her eyes, usually bright with curiosity, now reflected the burdens of someone twice her age.

"I looked for work in Hungary as a nurse for months but I couldn't find anything that would pay much or would use my skills. Then I was approached by this man, Andreas. He told me they needed nurses in America and that he could arrange my passage. I could even become a citizen." She looked down at her hands. "I know now how stupid I was to believe him, but the idea of being a real nurse here and making money to send back to my mother was wonderful."

"I can imagine," said Hans. He continued to listen as her words tumbled one on top of the other.

"From the moment I left Hungary, I knew it was a mistake. But I had already taken their money and used it to buy food and medicine for my mother. They brought me to Dr. Cesero's when we arrived. From the start, he paid me very little, but there was nothing I could do. He said the remainder was to pay for my immigration papers. About a month ago, he told me I was close to getting my green card. But earlier today after he was shot, I went into his office and found my passport and the passports of several other women still in his desk. Now I doubt he has done anything. You probably think me foolish for being so naïve."

Hans reached over and covered her hands with his. "Not at all. I think you're very brave."

Sasha gave him a dubious look as Hans's cellphone buzzed. He checked the screen. It was Robert.

"I have to get this," he told her.

"I left you a message at the hospital. Whenever you can check," said Robert when Hans answered. He could tell by Robert's tone they needed to be careful communicating.

"Thanks," Hans said, then powered off his cellphone. "I think it's best we leave our phones off," he told Sasha.

"I turned mine off before I went to meet you at the hospital," she replied. "Who was that?"

"Robert, my friend in British Intelligence. He left a message for me on my hospital voicemail."

Sasha nodded, her eyes growing wide. "Alina must have told the Russians about me. That's why the man went to my place. I'm putting you in danger by being here."

"Alina knows about me, too, and probably considers me a liability," Hans reminded her. "I need to get us a burner phone so I can check my voicemail, and I imagine you'd like to call your mother. There's a cellphone store nearby." He got up and grabbed his keys. "I would say you could come with me, but I don't think we should be seen together."

Sasha nodded. "I'll be fine."

"Lock up behind me."

When he got to the store a few minutes later, he found a long line of customers and only one salesclerk. He was going to be here for quite some time.

After Hans left, Sasha cleaned up the kitchen, then sat down in the living room and checked out the titles of the books on the coffee table. Most were about the brain, but there were some books on general medical topics. She picked up one volume on human anatomy, a well-worn reference with multiple pages turned down at the corners. She imagined Hans had owned the book since university. She opened it to see he had made numerous notations in the margins and ran her fingers lightly over the words. As she read his meticulous notes, she was struck by the exactitude of his thinking. Then she thought of the current situation and realized how out of control and unsettling this must be for him.

When it was finally Hans's turn in line, nearly an hour

had gone by. He told the salesclerk, "I'd like a disposable phone." The young man reached under the counter and pulled out an entire tray of phones. Hans picked up a small one that would easily fit in his pants pocket. "This looks good."

"You want a prepaid plan?" asked the clerk.

"Will it be untraceable?"

"You pay cash, yeah, it's untraceable. That'll be three hundred dollars."

Hans pulled out his wallet and handed him three bills.

"You've got four hundred domestic minutes and thirty international," said the clerk, handing him the phone.

When Hans was back in his car, he powered on the cell and dialed the hospital voicemail. He tapped his finger on the steering wheel as he listened to a lengthy message from a drug sales rep, then Robert's voice came on the line.

"Old friend, you've got yourself in deep," said the message. "Cesero's clinic has been on the FBI's radar for some time, as he's associated with the Russian mafia. And your damsel in distress is now wanted by Interpol. It appears she's a person of interest in a recent murder at Cesero's clinic. I'm working on getting you an FBI contact, but this is bad, Hans, watch your back."

# 20

When Hans got back to his condo, he couldn't find Sasha. He felt a momentary stab of panic. Robert's words about the situation being very bad reverberated in his head, and he was reminded of just how much trouble he and Sasha were in. Then he saw the closed bathroom door. "It's me," he called out.

A second later, the door opened and Sasha stood there, her purse over her shoulder. "Maybe it's best if I leave. It's me they're after," she said. "I would feel terrible if something happened to you."

"Please don't. Cesero keeping you hostage like that was disgraceful. And from what you're telling me, there are many more women in peril. My friend knows someone in the FBI who may be able to help us. He's working on getting us connected." Hans pulled the small phone out of his pocket and handed it to her. "The guy I bought it from said we can use it for limited international calls. I paid cash, so it's untraceable."

Sasha looked at the phone in her hands, then back at Hans. "I can't thank you enough."

"You just did," he said, his eyes warm on hers. He gestured with his head. "Call your mother if you like. I'm going to scrounge up something for dinner."

Sasha stayed in the hallway and dialed her mother's number, waiting as the phone rang several times. Finally, her mother answered. "Sasha. Is everything alright?"

"No, it's not. Something has gone wrong here. It's too much for me to explain on the phone, but you might be in danger." Sasha paused to give the message time to sink in. "I am okay," she continued. "This is just a precaution, but I want you to go and stay with friends until I can figure this out." Sasha waited for her mother's reply.

"I can stay with my friend Natalya." Sasha heard fear in her mother's voice. "Sasha, please be careful."

"I promise, *Anya*. Please go to Natalya's, as quickly as possible. Give me her phone number, and I will check on you there."

When Sasha hung up a minute later, she stood up straighter, then walked into the kitchen, where she found Hans laying two hamburger patties onto a hot skillet. He glanced at her and smiled, giving Sasha the pleasant, warm feeling she'd come to like.

"Is your mother okay?" he asked, covering the skillet with a lid as hot grease began popping in the pan.

Sasha came to stand on the other side of the counter, facing him. "I told her to go to a friend's house until this is settled." She paused. "If it is ever settled."

Hans took a spatula out of a drawer and ventured to open the lid to the skillet, then carefully turned over the burgers. "There's always a solution to any problem," he said. "We'll get this worked out."

Sasha liked the way Hans thought, even if it didn't seem realistic. For the moment, her mother was safe, and the food smelled delicious. And even though Sasha knew she should be worried about her future, every time Hans smiled at her, she felt like things just might be alright, after all.

"Can I do anything to help?" she asked.

He pointed to a cupboard. "We'll have to use bread for buns, so you can get out a loaf, then ketchup from the fridge. I might have a tomato, too, and some lettuce." He stopped what he was doing and went to a nearby pantry and lifted an apron from its hook. He handed it to Sasha and waited as she slipped it over her head. Then he tied the strings in the back for her.

Sasha found everything and began cutting up vegetables, all the while thinking how this was a new experience for her. She and her mother had always lived alone together. Being in the kitchen with a man and cooking with him was something she could have only imagined. She suspected now that if she had tried to picture this before, her imagination wouldn't have done it justice.

After they finished eating, Sasha insisted on washing the dishes, so Hans retreated to the living room to check on his mother. Though he could call her directly, he wanted to ask the front desk first if everything was okay.

"Meadowbrook Village," answered a woman.

"This is Hans Wagner. I'm calling to check on my mother."

There was a moment of silence, then the woman said, "Dr. Wagner? Didn't I just speak to you?"

Hans sprang up off the couch. "No, I haven't called since yesterday. Someone else called?" Hans tried to keep the panic from his voice.

"About five minutes ago. To ask about your mother and check on visiting hours."

Warning bolts shooting through him, Hans asked, "What did you tell him?"

"That she was resting comfortably," the woman stuttered. "And I told him the visiting hours, but I thought that was an odd question, since you visit her all the time."

"Has anyone come in?"

"No, visiting hours were over when he called. Should we be concerned, Dr. Wagner?"

"Can you check on her?"

As he waited, Sasha came in from the kitchen. "My mother," he mouthed. When the nurse finally came back on the line and told him his mother was fine and tucked in for the night, he breathed a sigh of relief. "No one is to pay a call to my mother that isn't written on the list of visitors in her chart," he said. "Please make certain the other nurses are also aware. Do you understand?" Once she had assured him that no one would visit his mother without his approval, Hans hung up the phone.

"Is she alright?" asked Sasha.

"For the moment, but someone called pretending to be me."

Hans dialed Robert's number. "It's me," he said when Robert answered. "I just called to check on my mother.

Someone called right before me and asked about visiting hours. Should I get her out of there?"

"It shouldn't be you," said Robert. "They're trying to smoke you out. Is there anyone nearby who can bring her to a safe place?"

"Yes," said Hans, who hung up and dialed the hospital. When his colleague Chuck came on the line, Hans said, "I need a favor."

"Sure."

"I had to leave town on an emergency. My mother is at Meadowbrook and experiencing stomach pains. Can you send someone to pick her up and bring her into the hospital? Then set her up in a room?"

"I'll get that started. When will you be back?"

"I'll let you know. Can you also make the staff aware she's to have no visitors? No exceptions, except me and you."

"Sure."

Hans called Meadowbrook Village again, dialing his mother's direct line this time. Her voice was groggy from sleep. "Hans, what's wrong?"

"This is for your own safety, so listen carefully. I am having someone pick you up and take you to the hospital in a few minutes. Give them the excuse your stomach hurts."

"This sounds serious, Hans. What's going on?"

"I can't explain right now. I just need you to trust me."

"I have complete faith in you, son," his mother said.

## 21

When Hans hung up the phone, he felt his hands shaking. If the Russians knew where his mother and Sasha lived, they likely knew where he lived.

"I think it's best we leave," he said.

"Where will we go?"

"We can check into a hotel. Let me just pack a few things." Hans went into his bedroom, his anxiety on overdrive as he pulled out a suitcase and began throwing clothes in. When he was in the bathroom filling up his toiletry bag, he felt his phone buzz.

"It's Chuck. Your mom is enroute. Want me to do some tests when she arrives?"

"If you can just keep her under observation that would be great," said Hans. "It could just be bad indigestion, but I want to make sure."

"Whatever you want," said Chuck.

"Thanks, I owe you."

The knowledge that his mother would soon be safe calmed his nerves. Hans stopped to think what else he needed for their escape. He went to his floor safe and pulled out the gun. When he stood up, Sasha walked into the room. She looked at the gun in his hand and her eyes widened.

"Robert insisted I get this years ago. I've only fired it a few times at a gun range," Hans said. "I never thought I'd need it." He stopped talking. The enormity of what faced them felt hard and cold, like the gun in his hand.

Sasha looked at the gun Hans clutched and felt an overwhelming urge to somehow assure him. But what could she possibly say? She reached out and gently took the gun from his hand, then set it on his bedside table. She came closer, and when he reached toward her, she took his hand and looked up at him. They stood that way for some time, gazing into each other's eyes. Sasha heard traffic swooshing by in the street below. Then Hans cupped his hands on the sides of her face and pulled her to him. When their lips met, Sasha felt lightheaded. She clung to him as they kissed, until the doorbell rang, forcing them apart. Hans grabbed the gun and headed for the front door while Sasha followed.

There were voices in the hallway. Sasha heard a woman say, "Keep it down. I have a baby sleeping."

"I'm looking for the person who lives here," said a man's voice.

"He's not home," the woman said, then a door slammed.

Hans put his finger to his lips, then readied the gun. Sasha wanted to look through the peephole but didn't dare. She watched the doorknob, expecting it to turn, but after a few more seconds, footsteps in the hallway retreated. Hans peered through the peephole, then pointed to his bedroom.

Once there, he asked, "Did that sound like one of the men in Cesero's office?"

"Yes, the man with the gun."

"We've got to get out of here," said Hans. "There's a gym downstairs with access to the back parking lot. He glanced out the bedroom window. "The darkness will give us some cover." Hans put the gun in his bag while Sasha got her purse. Then he opened his door and checked the hallway. No one in sight.

After taking the stairs to the basement, they headed through the gym's double doors. The room was vacant. "I'll go out first and bring the car around," Hans told her.

Sasha nodded in agreement. Though she remained aware of her surroundings as she waited, she couldn't help but think about their kiss, which still lingered on her lips.

A few minutes later, a car pulled up outside. Sasha let out a breath when she saw Hans emerge from the driver's side. He waved her out to the car. Soon they were headed away from his condominium complex.

"I'm thinking we go a few towns over to be safe," Hans said.

Just then, Sasha realized something. "How will we pay for the hotel?"

Hans turned his blinker on and took a right. "I have plenty of room on my credit card." Then he slammed a hand against the steering wheel. "We can't use my card. They'll track us. I don't have much cash."

"I have several thousand hidden at my apartment," said Sasha, without looking at him.

Hans glanced at her. "You do?"

"It's the money to buy my freedom from Dr. Cesero," she said, realizing how strange the words sounded out loud.

"I don't want to use your money, Sasha. Besides they're probably watching your apartment."

"I'll have to sneak in. What choice do we have?"

"I guess so." Hans strummed the steering wheel as they waited for a light to change. "I'll go in. They'll be less likely to notice. You can tell me where the money is."

Hans was right. They could easily mistake him for a resident of the complex. She gave him directions to her apartment and pulled out her key.

As they drove to Sasha's place, Hans played out how he'd get in and out of Sasha's apartment quickly. He didn't want to leave her in the car alone any longer than necessary. When they pulled up and he shut off the engine, he assured her, "I'll be quick." Then he got the gun out of his bag and put it in his pocket and headed to the far end of the complex. He would climb the stairs there and loop around to her apartment.

When he got to her door, he found it unlocked. He slowly turned the knob, listening intently. Silence. He slipped in and shut the door behind himself, bolting it and praying there was no one in there with him. He turned on the flashlight on his cellphone and shined the light around. A studio apartment. Simply furnished and orderly, except for mail lying on the floor of the threshold. Then he saw the telltale sign of a boot print on a white floor rug.

Working quickly, he climbed on her bed and pushed open the ceiling tile, then felt around until he came in contact with a leather pouch. He glanced around for an overnight bag and found one hanging from the back of her closet. Then he pulled items of clothing from hangers, swept blindly through a bureau drawer with lingerie, and stuffed it all in the bag. In the bathroom, he threw in some toiletries, and at the last minute he saw a pair of leather sandals on the floor and took those, too. He was walking out when the flashlight illuminated an envelope on the floor with foreign stamps on it. He picked it up and glanced at the return address. Hungary. After slipping the envelope into the bag, he let himself out and locked the door behind him. From the other end of the complex, he descended the stairs and quickly made his way to the car. When he slid behind the steering wheel, he handed the bag and pouch to Sasha, then backed out of the parking space.

"Someone was in your apartment. The door was unlocked, and I saw a boot print," he said as he checked the rearview mirror to make sure they weren't being followed. Out of the corner of his eye, he saw Sasha pull out the envelope from among her things.

"This is from my mother," she said, then tore it open.

Hans merged into the fast lane on the freeway as Sasha gasped. He glanced at the photo she held in her hands "The woman in the photo looks familiar," he said. "Who is she?"

"Her name is Anna," Sasha barely breathed out the words. "Hans, she's the woman in the coma."

## 22

When Sasha stared at Anna's face and realized how close she'd been to her, she felt overwhelmed and helpless. If only she'd received the photo earlier, but then what? She'd been powerless since the moment she had accepted Andreas's help.

"How do you know her?" asked Hans.

"She is the daughter of my mother's friend Natalya. My mother sent me her photo because she came to America before I did. Natalya hadn't heard from her since she left, until a phone call that got cut off last week. She told her mother she was in Los Angeles. They thought I might be able to locate her."

Hans drove in front of a hotel and stopped the car. "May I?" he asked, putting his hand out for the photo. Sasha gave it to him, and he took a closer look. "This was taken a few years ago, but it's definitely the young woman in the clinic. At least she is alive." He appeared thoughtful as he handed Sasha the photo. "Maybe we can find her."

Sasha was surprised at his words. "How would we do that?"

"I don't know, but clearly she needs help."

Sasha looked into Anna's eyes and imagined her mother's anguish since she left. She touched the girl's cheek and thought of her own mother being in the same situation and felt guilt wash through her.

"I'm going to check us in. I can get two rooms, if you want," said Hans, breaking into her thoughts.

"That would be expensive," said Sasha. "One room is fine." What Sasha failed to add was that she didn't want to be separated from Hans—not even for the night.

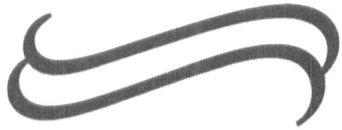

When the hotel clerk asked for Hans's credit card, he had to come up with something quick. "We've been traveling since early this morning, and someone lifted my wallet when we were in this little convenience store. They were slick, I have to give them that. I didn't feel a thing. I do have plenty of cash to cover my stay." He pulled out some hundred-dollar bills to show the clerk.

"I'll have to check with the manager." The man picked up the phone. When he hung up, he said, "I'm going to need a deposit for the room and payment for tonight up front."

"No problem," said Hans, glad that at least they had a place to stay. He handed the clerk the cash and took the room keycard.

"Third floor," said the clerk. "Parking is in the back of the building."

After they parked and took the elevator upstairs, Hans let them into their suite, a two-room affair with a back bedroom and front living room and a kitchenette. Hans set down their things.

"Very nice," said Sasha, looking around at the soft white walls, blond furniture and apricot-colored bedspread. A dish of chocolates sat on the bed-table.

"Excuse me," said Hans. "I need to check in at the hospital." He sat down at a small table next to the kitchenette and made the call.

"Hans. I've got your mother in a room," said Chuck when he came on the phone. "From what I can tell, she's fine."

"Thank you. I'm still in the middle of something, and I need another couple favors."

"Go on."

"Can you keep my mother there for a while longer? I'm working on getting someone to pick her up. I also need a few days off. Any way you can cover for me?"

"I should be able to take care of your shifts. Whatever I can't, I'll find someone. Is everything okay?"

Hans glanced at Sasha. "Everything will be okay. I just need a few days. I'll pick up the rest of the holidays for the year for you."

Sasha could tell by the uncomfortable look on Hans's face that evading didn't come easy to him. When he hung up, she asked, "How is your mother?"

The question caused his shoulders to relax. "She's doing well."

"That's some good news," said Sasha.

Hans smiled and yawned. "It's late. Maybe we should get some sleep."

Sasha nodded. "I'm going to take a shower first."

"Of course."

She took her things into the bathroom and closed the door, then stood staring at herself in the mirror. Her cheeks were flushed, and it wasn't because of their precarious situation. Sasha couldn't stop thinking about their kiss and wondering what would have happened if they hadn't been interrupted.

After Hans heard the shower go on, he ventured to imagine how lovely Sasha must look under the water. His burner phone buzzed then. An international number. He pressed answer.

"Have you gotten yourself somewhere safe?" It was Robert.

"Yes, and my mother is in the hospital."

"Good. I finally got ahold of that FBI contact. Her name is Savannah Sanchez. I set up the meet for you tomorrow morning at ten. You'll have to drive to Orange County. There's a nursery in Corona Del Mar by the name of Roger's Gardens."

"How will I spot her?"

"She'll find you. You're with Sasha?"

"Yes."

Robert was silent on the other end of the phone, then he cleared his throat. "Please be careful, Hans."

Hans could hear the worry in his friend's voice. "I'll be

fine," he assured him. As he hung up, he hoped he could live up to his promise.

When Sasha came out after showering, she wore a pink cotton nightgown, her long brown hair wet and glistening. "All yours." She gestured to the bathroom with her hairbrush.

"I just got a call from Robert. We have a meeting in Orange County tomorrow morning with the FBI agent."

"That's good," said Sasha as she ran the brush through her hair.

Hans watched for a moment, then said, "Well, I'm going to take that shower now." Feeling slightly silly about stating the obvious, he went into the bathroom and turned on the water. He let the warm water cascade over him until his muscles relaxed. Standing beneath the water for several minutes, eyes closed, he tried to slow his mind down. For now, they were safe.

When he came out a few minutes later, Sasha was lying curled up on the couch. He went and stood over her. "I can sleep here, and you can take the bed," he said.

She sat up and pushed stray tendrils of hair from around her face. "I'm okay here."

"I'd rather you took the bed," he said. "I don't mind."

"You'll be more comfortable in the bed. It's actually pretty comfy here."

Hans continued to stare at Sasha, every fiber in him wanting to kiss her. "Well, goodnight then," he said.

As he turned to go into the bedroom, Sasha called after him, "Hans?"

He turned around to meet her eyes. "Yes?"

She looked down at her hands, then back into his face. "I just want to thank you again. If it weren't for you, I don't know what would have happened to me by now."

Drawn by the vulnerability in her tone, Hans returned to the couch and knelt beside her, taking her hands in his. "Like

I told you. No need to thank me." He brought her hands to his mouth and kissed the top of each one gently. As he did so, Sasha leaned toward him ever so slightly, and Hans took that as a cue to kiss her. It was a long, deep kiss that had his heart pounding. When they finally pulled apart, Hans breathed, "Would you like to come to the bedroom with me?"

At his words, Sasha's body stiffened. Hans sat back on his heels, searching her face for clues as to what she was thinking. He saw a mix of emotions. "I'm sorry. I didn't mean to push," he said finally, starting to stand.

Sasha reached out and put her hand on his forearm. "I want to. I do, but..."

"It's not the right time," replied Hans.

"That's not it," she said, her voice barely above a whisper, her brown eyes earnest. "I've never been with a man before."

# 23

When Sasha admitted her inexperience, Hans looked at her with such surprise, her heart fell. "I'm not as experienced as you might have thought," she said, sadness washing through her.

Hans smiled and gently traced her cheek with his forefinger. "No need to apologize, you're absolutely perfect. Are you sure?"

Sasha saw the genuine warmth in his eyes and felt safer than she'd ever felt. "Yes, I do want to go to the bedroom with you."

To Sasha's delight, Hans responded by picking her up and carrying her into the bedroom, the side of her body pressed against his broad chest, still moist from the shower. When they stood next to the bed, he gently lifted her nightgown up and over her head, Sasha's body quivering in a most appealing way. She gasped when he put his hands on her bare bottom and brought his lips to hers, his chest hairs caressing her nipples, sensitive with desire.

While their first kiss had been long and intense, this one

felt hot. When their lips pulled apart, he took her hands and placed them on the drawstring of his sweatpants. Keeping his eyes on hers, he nodded slightly. Sasha untied the string and eased the pants over his hips. Then he guided her hands onto his penis. Its firmness pulsated beneath her fingertips, sending a flush of deep desire throughout her body. He showed her how to stroke him, which she did, feeling him become even larger in her hands. Then he eased her back on the bed and spread her legs and began exploring her private area with his fingers. When she was gasping in delight and wet with need, he straddled her. "This may be uncomfortable," he said. "If at any time you want me to stop, just tell me."

Awash with desire for Hans and unable to speak, Sasha nodded as he entered her. He was right, it did hurt at first, but then she was overcome with a sensation like nothing she'd ever experienced. She felt at one with Hans, like a part of his skin. She wanted him to possess her completely. Then as waves of pleasure washed through her, she found herself saying his name. Soon after, Hans also cried out. When they finished, and Sasha lay panting beneath him, her body limp and satisfied, he reached over for the tissue box and handed it to her. Sasha had known to expect the blood that came with the first time, but she was shocked at how red it appeared. She threw the tissue in the trash can, then nestled next to Hans, who lay staring at the ceiling.

"That was beautiful, Sasha," he said, pulling her tight to him and stroking her hair. "Are you okay? No regrets?"

Overcome with an emotion she couldn't have described if she tried, Sasha nodded against his chest. "It was wonderful," she finally managed to whisper. "Much better than I ever imagined."

Hans kissed the top of her head, then continued to stroke her hair for a time. Before long, she heard him softly snoring.

Sasha snuggled even closer against him, her heart overflowing with something that could only be happiness.

Hans stirred in the middle of the night to find he and Sasha still intertwined. Her breath caressed the side of his chest. He thought of the danger they were in and an urge to protect her at all costs swept through him. He had known many women, but she was the first he would lay down his life for. The realization both excited and scared him.

When Hans awoke in the morning, he looked through the doorway to see Sasha filling the coffee maker, her long brown hair hiding her face. He checked the clock on the bedside table. Eight a.m.

Sasha walked into the room then. "Good morning," she said, her smile reaching all the way to her eyes. He hoped he had something to do with that.

"Did you have a good night's sleep?" she asked.

Hans reached out a hand for hers and pulled her onto the bed. "Better than I have in years. Lie down with me while the coffee percolates. How did you sleep?"

"Great," she said, cuddling next to him. Hans marveled at how well they fit. They stayed that way until the scent of coffee wafted to them. "I wish we could stay here, but we need to go meet the FBI contact," he said.

Sasha sighed. "I need to get ready."

. . .

Thirty minutes later, they were making their way south to Orange County. Sasha was quiet at first, then suddenly burst out, "There were other women who came to America when I did."

Hans glanced at her, then back at the road. "Other nurses?"

"No, I was the only nurse. The other girls didn't have particular skills that I know of, but they were very pretty."

Hans knew there was no delicate way to say what he said next. "So, they had to work off their passage in a different way?"

Sasha nodded and looked as if she might cry.

"What happened to them?"

"A car picked them up when we docked in Los Angeles, and I never saw them again. Alina took only me to Dr. Cesero's. And..." The memories seemed to be painful to Sasha. "There was a pregnant girl on the ship. I assisted with the birth of her baby."

The more Hans learned of what Sasha had endured, the more furious he became. "What happened to her?"

Sasha put her head in her hands and choked back a sob. "I don't know. When we docked, she didn't get off the ship. Alina sold the baby to a man and a woman waiting for her on the dock."

"Good God!" said Hans, who had taken his eyes off the freeway too long and had to swerve out of the way of a car. He couldn't believe what he was hearing.

Sasha turned to look at him. "You must think I'm a terrible person now."

Hans glanced at a sign as they went by. Three more exits. "Hold on a minute," he said, willing himself to focus on driving. He got off at their exit and pulled into a grocery store parking lot. Sasha was looking away from him out the window. "Look at me," he said softly.

She turned, her cheeks wet with tears. He reached for a fast-food napkin stuck in the console and handed it to her. "Why on earth would I think of you as a terrible person?"

"Because I didn't do anything about the other girls."

"You did what you needed to protect yourself and your mother. And you've kept going. That shows great courage. Now let's go see the FBI agent. She can hopefully get us safely out of this situation."

He turned the car engine on and eased out of the parking lot, praying that he was right.

## 24

When they pulled into Roger's Gardens and stopped the car, Hans eyed the entrance. Potted palms flanked the walkway and hanging baskets overflowed with brightly colored flowers.

"How curious that the contact wanted to meet here," said Sasha as they got out of the car.

"I was just thinking the same thing." Hans glanced around as they headed through the entrance. They walked down a path alongside tables covered in potted herbs and vegetables. When they came to the rosebushes, Hans stopped to admire a vivid, pink-colored bloom.

"They make the roses look beautiful nowadays but they breed out the fragrance," said a voice behind them with a Southern twang.

Hans and Sasha turned around to face a tall, willowy blond wearing a dark blue suit and silver hoop earrings. When she stuck out her hand to shake theirs, Hans spied a gun holstered under her jacket.

"Savannah Sanchez," she said, her grip firm. Then she pointed a manicured finger at a rosebush with bright red blooms. "That one is Mr. Lincoln. An old rose with a wonderful scent." She laughed. "Apologies for the garden lecture. My mama and gramma run a nursery back in Georgia." She gestured to a vine-covered gazebo a short distance away. "What say we go over there and talk."

When they were all sitting under the gazebo, Savannah's manner turned more serious. "Robert filled me in as much as he could, but I need to hear from you," she said, directing her attention at Sasha.

Sasha wasn't sure what to make of the woman now staring her down. She'd never met an FBI agent, and she wasn't sure just how much she should tell her.

As if the woman could read Sasha's mind, she said, "I need the whole story, Sasha. You're wanted for questioning in a murder. Normally, I'd bring you in immediately, but as a favor to Robert, I'm not. Yet."

Swallowing the fear in her throat when Savannah mentioned murder, Sasha gave her the highlights of what had occurred over the last few days. As she talked, Hans piped in to add how Alina had forced him at gunpoint to treat Anna.

Sasha reached into her purse for the envelope from her mother, then pulled out the photo of Anna and handed it to Savannah. "This is the woman known as Madeline, but her real name is Anna Rosko, from Budapest. I believe she's being held against her will here. You can keep the photo if it will help."

Savannah slid the photo into her jacket pocket. "This Alina. Do you know her last name?"

Sasha shook her head. "She never said."

Savannah turned to Hans. "Where did she abduct you? The hospital parking lot? We might be able to pull some footage and ID her."

"It was in the staff area of the parking garage. There are cameras, but she was wearing sunglasses and a scarf."

Savannah took a small notebook out and nodded as she jotted things down. "It's still worth looking at that footage." She tapped the pen on the book. "I think Robert told you that we've been monitoring Eastern European syndicate activity in the area for some time. Cesero's name was on the watch list. You both were closer than we've been able to get. It would help if we could get a sketch of Alina. We'll send an artist to the safe house I'm going to send you to."

"I have a request," said Hans. "They threatened my elderly mother, Gretchen Wagner, in her care facility, so I had her transported to Mercy General, the hospital where I work. Can the FBI get her out of there and to safety?"

"I can arrange for her to go to one of our LA safe houses. You two are going to a house not far from here." She gave them directions and the combination to the key lockbox, then took down Hans's cell number. "Let's leave separately," she said. Then she got up and walked briskly away.

Sasha and Hans waited a few minutes, then went to his car. When he started to punch the address of the safe house into the GPS, Sasha stopped him. "We don't want any record of where we're going."

Hans stopped entering the address in the GPS. He reached over and opened the glovebox. "I think I have an ancient map of Southern California in here somewhere." After he fished it out, they located their destination up the coast in Huntington Beach.

Before long, they pulled into the driveway of a small, unassuming cottage several blocks from the beach. When they got out of the car, the salt air and sound of seagulls greeted them. They walked through a short entryway into the house. A smattering of beach-themed art decorated the living room walls, complimenting the room's sea-blue sofa. In the back, they found a small kitchen with a faucet dripping. Sasha walked over and turned the handles. Then she opened the cupboards to find boxed meals and canned goods. The refrigerator had some water bottles, juice boxes, and butter.

"Are you hungry?" she asked.

"Not particularly," said Hans. "You?"

"No." She noticed a round, brown stain on the white Formica countertop.

Hans moved closer to her. "Besides the obvious, what's the matter?"

She sighed. "Once this is all over, which I hope happens soon, I'll have to go back to Budapest." What she didn't add to the end of her sentence was, "without you."

Hans knew what Sasha was saying—that before long she'd have to go home, and they'd be separated. That wasn't something he wanted. Before he could respond to the look of sadness in Sasha's eyes, a knock on the door jarred him back to reality.

"Who could that be?" Sasha whispered, her eyes anxious.

Hans had left the gun in his bag in the living room. "Hopefully the sketch artist, but let me go see first." He hurried to the living room and pulled the gun out. Then he quietly approached the door as someone rapped again and a woman's voice said, "Savannah sent me."

Gun in one hand, Hans peeked through the spy-hole to see a woman standing in front of the door holding up an FBI badge. He slipped the gun in the back of his pants and opened the door.

"I'm Agent Sullivan," said a short, compact woman with a head full of springy, black curls. "You must be Mr. Wagner."

Hans nodded and let her in. Then he closed and bolted the door. "We're in the kitchen," he said, pointing toward the back.

"This is Agent Sullivan," said Hans to Sasha. He gestured to the kitchen table. "Will this space work for the sketch?"

"It'll work great," she said, pulling out a chair. "Can you turn on the overhead lights?" The woman then took out a sketchpad and a small case of charcoal pencils. "There are computer programs for sketching nowadays," she said, "but I prefer old school for the original artwork. We scan the results and put them into our databases. Let's start with the face shape of the woman you know as Alina. Would you say it's round? Or thin and narrow?"

As the agent worked on the drawing, Sasha seemed to gradually relax. After about thirty minutes, the agent had drawn a good representation of Alina. She took a photo of it with her cellphone. "I'm sending this to see if the system picks anything up on our mystery woman." Within minutes, her phone pinged and she glanced at the text. "Looks like we already have an ID. Alina Bakós. Hungaro-Slovak Mafia. She works with a brother. Interpol has them both listed as wanted for trafficking and extortion. We haven't identified him yet."

"I can identify him," said Sasha. "He's the reason I'm here. His first name is Andreas."

## 25

The agent sat up straighter and scrutinized Sasha for a moment. "You're telling me you were trafficked by the Bakós siblings and you escaped? They're known for being merciless."

Sasha looked down at the table and shifted in her seat, feeling uncomfortable with the question. "I guess I was lucky. My nursing skills saved me."

Agent Sullivan took the sketchpad out again and placed it on the table. "You must be very resourceful." She looked at Sasha. "Shall we begin to work on a sketch of Andreas?"

"If it will stop him, yes." Sasha leaned forward. "He has a lean face, like Alina's. I can't believe I didn't see the resemblance before. Although, he has dark brown, almost black eyes, and hers are a lighter gray color."

Agent Sullivan began sketching. "They would have some dissimilarities. According to our intel, they share the same father but different mothers. And their father is high-level in the syndicate."

That explained why Alina always acted as if she was invincible, thought Sasha.

. . .

Thirty minutes later, they had a good likeness of Andreas. Agent Sullivan shot a photo and sent it to Savannah. Then she sat back in her chair. "Is there anything else you can give me on the Bakós sibling's operations?"

"Let me get us some water," Hans said, returning with three bottles.

After Sasha took a long drink, she told her story. "I was skeptical about coming to America," she said, "but Andreas was persistent. We met several times so he could answer my questions. All lies, I know now, except for the part about me using my nursing skills here." She paused and took another drink of water. She was embarrassed to admit how gullible she had been.

"The usual story is girls are enticed with the promise of modeling. But then they are trafficked for sex," said Agent Sullivan. "Although we have encountered similar stories as yours involving doctors and other skilled professionals, including people with financial and computer skills. The end result is always the same, though. Once the person is no longer useful, the traffickers get rid of them. That makes your case unusual."

Sasha put her head in her hands, thinking about Anna and her fate.

"I don't mean to upset you," said Agent Sullivan.

Sasha raised her head. "It's not me, it's Anna and all the other women they're holding captive. They have also threatened my mother in Budapest."

"We don't have jurisdiction in Budapest, unfortunately. I'm told you instructed her to go somewhere safe?"

"She's with Anna's mother, but I don't know how safe that is."

Agent Sullivan gathered her things. "I'm not making any

promises, but if you agree to testify when Alina and Andreas are apprehended, we might be able to arrange some protection for your mother. The U.S. does have good relations with Hungary. You would need to check that out with Savannah, though." She stood and put out her hand to shake Sasha's. "It's very brave of you to come forward like this. These are very dangerous people. It's vital that you stay in the safe house while we work to apprehend them."

Once the agent left, Hans put his arms around Sasha and drew her to him, then guided them both to the couch. They stayed that way for a long time, the house quiet, except for the tick of a clock on the wall. Hans thought about the last few days and how much his life had changed. Though the situation was perilous, he felt oddly at peace. He was supposed to be with Sasha. He knew that now. And there was an obvious way to ensure that remained the case.

He was about to tell Sasha his idea when his phone buzzed in his pocket. He pulled it out and checked the screen. An international number.

When Sasha took the phone, she was afraid to say anything, so she just waited. Then her mother said, "Sasha?"

"It's me, *Anya*. Did you get safely to Natalya's?"

"I did, but she's not here. Her son, Mihai, says Natalya got a call yesterday about Anna. She left in a hurry and hasn't come back. What is going on, Sasha?"

Alarm bells clanging in Sasha's head, she tried to keep her voice level. "It's a long story, *Anya*. I saw Anna a few days ago, and she was okay."

"You did! That's wonderful. Natalya will be so relieved. Is Anna with you?"

"No, but there are people looking for her to bring her home safely. Does anyone know you are at Natalya's?"

"I told no one. But when I got here, Natalya was gone. What should I do?"

"Don't leave the house unless you have to, and don't let anyone in. I'll get back to you soon."

When Sasha hung up the phone, she filled in Hans. The hysteria she had been tamping down while talking to her mother bubbled to the surface now. She began pacing and wringing her hands. "I know the FBI said to stay here, but I feel I should go back to Budapest to protect my mother."

Hans got off the couch and came to stand in front of her. "I don't think that's a good idea, but if you insist, I'll go with you." He paused. "First, we need to do something. If you're in agreement with it."

Sasha couldn't think of anything more important than getting on a flight to Budapest immediately. "What is it?" She watched as the expression on Hans's face became thoughtful.

"I know time is of the essence, but your passport is currently flagged by Interpol. As soon as you show it at the airport, they'll arrest you."

Hans was right. Tears of frustration pricked at the back of her eyes. "I can't just sit here while Andreas is looking for my mother!"

"Please hear me out."

"I'm listening."

"I happen to know a very wealthy man who owns a private jet. I did brain surgery on his son several years ago and removed a tumor. He said if I ever needed anything to call him. I think he could fly us to Hungary under the radar."

Sasha couldn't believe her ears. She felt a surge of hope. "That would be wonderful. And you would go with me?"

"Yes, but realize once there, you'd have to stay in Hungary."

At the meaning of his words, Sasha felt a sadness fill her chest.

Hans took a breath and continued. "I know we haven't known each other all that long. And I always thought the idea of love at first sight was a misnomer. But the truth is, Sasha"—Hans seemed to search for words—"I want you in my life." He took her hands in his. "Let's get married before we leave the country."

Sasha thought she must have heard Hans incorrectly. "What?"

"You mean everything to me," said Hans, who began walking about the room as if he gained clarity from moving. He came back to where Sasha stood. "If we get married before we leave, you'll be able to return to the United States as my wife."

"But Hans, you can't do that," Sasha practically stuttered.

"I want to, Sasha," he said, his expression sincere. He took a step back. "But I realize this is very quick. If you aren't sure, I understand."

At that moment, it hit Sasha that Hans was serious. That more than wanting to help her, he sincerely wanted her. So profound was the realization that she felt like crying and laughing at the same time. She loved being with Hans and couldn't imagine anything she wanted more than to always be part of his life. But to be his wife. She never imagined that. Her feelings for him could not be truer, and she believed it was love in his eyes when he looked at her. Hans was a kind and honest man. Someone she could always count on. Yes, she wanted to spend her life with this man.

"Oh, Hans. I want that more than anything I've ever wanted!" She threw herself into his arms and reveled in the solid, safe warmth of his embrace. "But how, if we're trying to stay out of sight?"

"I have an idea," said Hans as they pulled apart. "It'll require calling in a few more favors." He flipped open the phone and sat down on the couch.

After Hans called the billionaire, who agreed to have his jet ready and waiting, he dialed Robert.

"Tell me you're safe," said his friend.

"For now, but there's been a development. Sasha's mother is in danger. We need to go to Hungary."

"Hans, that's crazy."

"You've gotten into crazy things over the years, and I've always supported you," said Hans.

"Point taken. What can I do?"

"I'm going to need alias passports for us," Hans said, then walked into the next room and added in a low voice, "And someone to marry us before we leave. We'll get the legal marriage certificate at the courthouse, but it'd mean a lot to have even a quick ceremony. I was hoping Helga could make it special for us."

"Bloody hell! Now I know you've lost your mind."

When Hans didn't respond, Robert's tone softened. "I'll call Helga to make the arrangements."

"Thank you, old friend," said Hans. "And before you say it,

I promise I'll be careful." Hans gave Robert the address of the private airport and hung up.

"We need to go to the courthouse to get our marriage certificate right away," he told Sasha. At the look of worry on her face, he said, "I know this exposes us, but we'll make it quick. By tonight, we'll be on our way to Hungary."

As they prepared to leave, Hans's cellphone buzzed. It was Savannah.

"Are you settled in okay?" she asked.

"Yes," lied Hans as he watched Sasha pull on a green sundress and gather her things to leave.

"Sit tight. I don't have news for you yet, but we're working all of the angles here."

"Will do," said Hans, then he put the phone in his pocket. He knew Savannah would explode when she realized they were gone. Hans barely recognized his life now. In college, while he watched people like Robert take all sorts of risks, he had been diligent about his studies. In medical school, science and medicine kept him grounded, clearheaded and with a purpose. But now, watching Sasha quickly brush through her beautiful hair and clasp it in a barrette, he realized that though he'd been driven to become a physician, his personal life had been passionless. Until now.

Sasha looked at him, her eyes lighting up with her smile. "Ready to go?"

"I am," said Hans, who took her bag and his.

Once in the car, Hans said, "Hopefully, we can get in and out of the courthouse quickly. I'm driving us to the next city over to play it safe with avoiding detection."

As Hans predicted, the process went smoothly. Within thirty minutes, they were back in the car with their marriage certificate, and another forty minutes later they pulled up to the private airstrip. It was late afternoon and the sun hung low in the sky. He spotted Helga standing near the hangar, waiting for them. The jet was already on the tarmac.

He and Sasha got out of the car, and Helga came toward them. "Hans, my boy, it's been a long time." The older woman's face lit up in a broad smile. Though her hair had a few more gray streaks since the last time he'd seen her, she had the same spring in her step he remembered. She wore a green caftan dress over her large, tall frame and held a small box in her hands.

Sasha turned toward Hans, surprise on her face.

"I wanted this to be more special than just a certificate," he explained.

Sasha stood on her tiptoes and kissed him twice on the mouth. "Thank you, for being, well, for being you," she said. Then she turned to Helga, who took Sasha's hands in hers.

"What a lovely lass you are. I'm Helga, dear, an old friend come to give this beautiful union a perfect beginning."

Sasha's face flushed as she smiled shyly at Helga. "Thank you. It's very nice to meet you."

"Well, I know we're on a time crunch, so we best get started," said Helga. "I wrangled the co-pilot to witness the ceremony. He's inside waiting." They all walked through the giant doors into the hangar, now empty, except for a circle of rose petals sprinkled in the center of the floor.

"Best I could do on such short notice," Helga said in Hans's ear. She turned to a muscular Black man in a pilot's uniform. He jutted out his hand to shake Hans's. "I'm Reginald Sampson. Mr. Magway speaks very highly of you, Dr. Wagner."

Hans shook his hand. "Very nice to meet you, Reginald. This is Sasha. We appreciate you agreeing to witness the ceremony."

"Shall we?" said Helga, gesturing for all to enter the circle of petals. She motioned Hans and Sasha to come face her. Reginald stood behind them.

"Normally, I get flowery when I do a ceremony," said Helga, laughing at her own joke. "Today, I'll make it short." She took a moment to smile warmly at the two of them. "We're gathered here today to join Hans Wagner and Sasha Farkas in holy matrimony. Should there be anyone who protests to their union, speak now." She paused for a millisecond. "Hans, do you take Sasha to be your wife? To honor and cherish her from this day forward, as long as you both shall live?"

"I do," said Hans, gazing at Sasha.

Then Helga turned to Sasha. "Sasha, do you take Hans to be your husband? To honor and cherish him from this day forward, as long as you both shall live?"

"I do," said Sasha. She looked into Hans's eyes as he held her hands in his.

Helga held up the box. "From what Robbie told me, there wasn't time to get rings, so I took the liberty. Hopefully they fit." She opened the box to reveal two gold wedding bands, one smaller than the other. "Wedding rings are a symbol of unbroken love and devotion," she continued. "Hans, please place Sasha's ring on her finger and give her your promise."

Hans took the smaller ring and while sliding it on Sasha's finger said, "With this ring, I promise to honor, love, and cherish you always."

Then Sasha took the other ring and slid it on his finger. When she finished, she said, her voice soft and low, "With this ring, I promise to honor, and cherish, and love you always."

"Well, then," said Helga. "I now pronounce you husband and wife. You may kiss the bride but make it snappy. I won't feel relaxed until you're off the ground."

Hans met Sasha's lips for their first kiss as husband and wife.

Then Helga handed them their alias passports. "These should get you safely into Hungary," she said. "And here's a credit card you can use that matches your aliases. Hopefully when you return, everything will be worked out and you can use your real passports."

"Thank you so much for doing this," Hans said.

Helga grasped his hands in hers. "You take care of yourself and your new bride. I know you mean the world to Robbie."

"I will," Hans promised. Then he and Sasha headed to board the plane. As they did so, a ripple of anxiety coursed through him. Was he being foolish heading straight for danger? Could he really keep his new bride safe?

## 27

They landed at Budapest International Airport in the midafternoon and disembarked to a silken heat, the sun bright overhead. In the terminal, an agent checked their passports and waved them through. "That was easy," said Sasha, who had expected a much more involved process.

"I think my billionaire friend greased a few palms," said Hans.

Sasha looked at him, confused.

Hans laughed. "It's an American expression. It means he paid a few people off to look the other way."

Sasha nodded knowingly. "Well, I would like to thank him one day." She glanced around the terminal. "Car rentals." She pointed to a sign.

They rented a silver Audi using the credit card Helga provided, then made their way to the lot. "Now it's my turn to ask a question," said Hans, when the attendant drove the car up and gave him the keys. "What side of the road do you drive on here?"

Sasha laughed. "The right side."

Once in the car, Hans pulled out the phone and powered

it on. "How about you check in with your mother before we get her?"

Sasha dialed Natalya's number and waited, but the phone just rang and rang. Panic pounded in her temples as she ended the call, then dialed again. "There's no answer," she said.

Hans steered them out of the parking lot. "There's likely an explanation," he said. "Try calling her again in a few minutes."

Sasha took a deep breath and set the phone in her lap. Hans was right. Her mother could just be in the bathroom. She gave him directions, and he headed toward downtown Budapest.

As they traveled, Hans glanced to the skyline punctuated by massive, ornate buildings. "What amazing architecture," he said. "Budapest is such a photogenic place, much more cosmopolitan than I expected. Doesn't the Danube run through the center of the city?"

"That's right," said Sasha. "Natalya lives on the Pest side, as does my mother. The Buda side is a little more upscale and not quite as lively as the Pest side." She dialed the phone again. "Still no answer," she said, her panic turning into terror.

Hans said nothing but kept up with the easy flow of traffic. If she wasn't so concerned about her mother, she would be more excited about being home after three years away. When they finally came to Natalya's neighborhood, she directed him to park on the cobblestone street. She pointed to a doorway two doors down where the porch was flanked by pots overflowing with red geraniums.

Hans reached into the back seat and took out the gun from his bag. "Let's go," he said. "Stay behind me."

When she got out of the car, Sasha stood on unsteady legs and tried to push down the fear at what they might see. After quickly crossing the street, Hans rapped on the door. When there was no answer, he tried the doorknob. It was open. They walked into a quiet hallway containing an ornate carpet runner that led past a stairway to the upper floor. Making their way in silence, they entered the kitchen. Empty. Sasha's heart clutched when she spied a spilled glass of water on the table. They continued into the living room, then Sasha cried out at the sight. A young man lay in the center of the room, unmoving.

Hans went to him and checked his pulse. "He's alive," he said. "Someone must have hit him. Try to revive him while I finish checking the place."

Hans left the room and Sasha heard him climbing the stairs. Though every fiber in her wanted to shout for her mother, Sasha did as he instructed. In the kitchen, she wet a towel with cool water and brought it to dab at the man's wound and then placed it on his forehead. Soon, he stirred and opened his eyes.

"Shh," she said. "I'm Sasha. You must be Natalya's son."

He nodded slightly. "Mihai," he managed to say.

"Is my mother here?" she asked him.

At the look of fear in his eyes, Sasha knew the answer.

"They took her," he said, grimacing in pain. "I tried to stop them."

Just then, Hans walked into the room. "No one else in the house," he said.

"This is Mihai, Natalya's son." Sasha stared up at Hans. "He said someone took my mother a little while ago. Was it a man or a woman?" she asked him.

"A man," he said.

"What age?" asked Sasha.

"About thirty-five or forty. He was Hungarian."

"Did he have a tattoo on his hand that looks like a spider?"

"Yes," said Mihai. "Do you know him?" He started to sit up, and Hans came to his side and helped lead him to the sofa.

"I'm a doctor," said Hans. "I'm going to check you out." He took the cellphone from his pocket and shined the light into the man's eyes. Then he inspected the gash. "Do you feel lightheaded, dizzy?"

"No." Mihai tried to sit up. "We must find our mothers."

"It will be better to stay where you are for now," said Hans. "It doesn't look like you have any permanent damage, but you can't be sure with head injuries."

Hans stood and pointed to the kitchen, and Sasha followed him in there. "Without having tools at my disposal, I can't say for sure if he doesn't have a more serious brain injury."

Sasha couldn't think straight. Then she said the words that she hoped she would never utter in the same sentence as her mother. "Andreas has my mother."

"Let's think this through," said Hans. "Is there anywhere you've seen him hanging out?"

"There's a coffee shop down the street where I used to meet him. But it's been three years since I was here. I doubt he would take my mother there."

Just then something crashed to the floor in the living room. They ran in to see both Mihai and a lamp on the floor by a nearby table. While Hans went to attend to him, Sasha heard a phone ringing in the kitchen. She went to the room and followed the sound to a purse on the table. Rummaging around, she found a cellphone and checked the screen. An unknown number. She answered but didn't say anything.

"Sasha, my dear, I know that's you. This is Andreas." Sasha heard someone moaning in the background. "I'm aware you are with your doctor friend. If he knows we are talking, I will kill your mother right now."

Sasha's breath caught.

"You and I have unfinished business. Come to me now, alone."

"I'll come," said Sasha in a low voice. "Please don't hurt her."

"That's what I like to hear," said Andreas. "I'll text you an address. Be here in twenty minutes."

As Sasha closed the phone and put it in her pocket, Hans walked in.

"Did I hear you talking to someone?"

She shook her head. "No, just muttering to myself. How is Mihai?"

"I think he's going to be okay. Let me tell him we're leaving to look for Andreas."

As soon as Hans began talking to Mihai again, Sasha hurried to the front door and pulled it open. She clicked the door shut softly behind her, then headed out on foot to Andreas and her mother.

# 28

Sasha rushed through the streets of Budapest, heart pounding against her ribcage as she pushed away visions of Andreas torturing her mother. When she arrived in District VIII, she checked the address. It was just ahead. She stopped in front of a rundown apartment building, the façade cracked and decayed. Once she went in, she worried she might not come out alive. She thought of Hans then and all he'd done for her. Quickly, before she could change her mind, she called Natalya's house.

He answered after one ring. "Hello?"

"Hans," said Sasha.

"Where are you?"

"I lied to you. I was talking to someone on my mother's phone. She left it at Natalya's, and Andreas called it. He has her, Hans."

"Why didn't you have me go with you?"

"He said I had to come alone or he would kill her."

"That bastard. Where are you?"

"Thank you for the last few days, Hans. I never thought I would be cared for by such a wonderful man."

"Sasha, please, don't. You're on a suicide mission. Let me come to you."

Swallowing back tears, Sasha hung up, then shoved the phone in her pocket and headed up the steps.

Hans dialed Robert's number. Before his friend had a chance to speak, Hans asked, "Can you trace a phone call for me?"

"What happened?"

"Sasha left to meet up with one of the traffickers. He called her on her mother's cellphone. They have the same last name. She lives in Pest."

"Okay, try to calm down. I might be able to trace it. Give me a moment. I'll call you right back."

When he hung up, Hans spun around to see Mihai standing in the doorway of the kitchen. "What happened?" he asked.

"Sasha got a call and left. They have her mother."

Mihai's eyes grew wide. "Maybe my mother is there, too."

"As soon as I find out where they are, we can call the police," Hans said.

"No police," said Mihai. "They can't be trusted."

"Then I'll go there myself," said Hans. "I have a gun."

"I'll go with you."

"You're injured. You should stay here and recover."

"I'll go," said Mihai.

"Fine," said Hans. He did need someone who knew the area.

Sasha tried the door, which opened. As she stepped into a dank hallway, the smell of urine assaulted her nostrils. A large lump leaning against the wall moved, and she jumped. Then her eyes adjusted to the light, and she saw it was an old man. He held a bottle in his hand.

"Is there someone else here?" she asked him in Hungarian.

He looked at her with a vacant expression, then took a drink from his bottle. She passed by him and headed for the back of the apartment. As she walked, the floor creaked. She stopped every few seconds and listened. Had she walked into a trap? She came to the kitchen, which looked like it hadn't been used in years. Beyond that, she saw a living room. Creeping along, her breath coming in short gasps, she headed for the room, then walked in. It held an old couch, the seat cushion gnawed on by rodents. Off the room was a hallway leading to bedrooms. The door to the first room was open. She peered inside. Just a mattress on the floor. A few steps farther and she came to the bathroom, empty and foul smelling. The last door was closed. She reached out to touch the knob when she felt a sharp pain on the back of her head, then everything went dark.

Hans pounced on the phone when it rang. "Did you get it?" he asked.

"Is this Sasha's doctor friend?" said a man's voice.

The muscles in Hans's neck tightened, and he barked, "Is this Andreas?"

"Sasha has spoken of me."

"If you harm her, I'll—"

Andreas cut him off. "Kill me? Many have tried and failed."

"What do you want?"

"For you to pay off Sasha's debt. Five hundred thousand dollars. It would have been much less if she didn't run away, but now there's interest."

Hans knew he needed to stall Andreas. "It's going to take me a little while to gather the money. Let me talk to her."

"She's not able to come to the phone right now." Then he hung up.

Hans slammed down Natalya's phone and began pacing. He couldn't get five hundred thousand dollars together that quickly. The phone rang again, and he grabbed it.

"Yes?"

"It's Robert. I just texted you an address in District VIII. If you can wait a few more hours, I could come help you."

"I can't wait," said Hans and hung up. He turned to Mihai. "Are you ready?"

Sasha gradually came to, as if crawling through a thick fog. She opened her eyes and rubbed the back of her head, which had a painful lump. Then she checked her pocket and found the phone was still there. She took it out to dial Hans and tell him she'd been tricked and her mother wasn't here,

139

but she heard footsteps outside the door. She stuffed the phone in her bra, then closed her eyes, feigning unconsciousness.

The footsteps grew louder as they entered the room. The tip of something hard, it felt like a boot, poked at her side, then kicked her over on her back. She suppressed a wince and kept her eyes closed.

"I know you're awake," said Andreas. "Open your eyes, or I'll do much more damage with my boot."

Sasha squinted to see him hovering over her, a sneer on his face.

"We were lenient with you, Sasha. We gave you freedoms most of the girls don't get, and this is how you repay us."

Sasha tried to scuttle away but Andreas reached down and grabbed her arm, yanking her to a standing position. His face inches from hers, his eyes dark brown slits flashing venom, he said, "Now you owe much more for your passage to America."

"I'm no longer in America."

He tightened his grip on her arm.

"Take me to my mother," Sasha demanded.

He laughed, the sound echoing in the empty room. Then he pulled her tight against him. "Not until you make a special payment that I should have taken a long time ago."

When Sasha tried to struggle free, he ripped the front of her blouse open. Then he saw the phone and snatched it. Letting go of her, he checked the phone log. "You've been making calls, I see. One to your doctor." He opened the phone and took out the SIM card and broke it in half. Then he threw the phone on the floor and stomped on it. Sasha turned her face away, loathing Andreas, her mind searching frantically for a plan to save her mother from an evil she didn't deserve.

## 29

Sasha tried to hold her blouse closed over her chest as Andreas dragged her out the back door and forced her into a van.

"Try to run, and your mother will pay the consequences," he snarled, then pulled the van door shut. Seconds later, he began driving.

"Where are you taking me?" Sasha asked quietly from the back.

"Where I should have taken you from the start." At a stoplight, Andreas punched a message into his phone, then threw it on the passenger seat.

Sasha was afraid to say anything else, but the panic she felt over her mother's abduction overrode her fear. "Where is my mother?"

Andreas looked back at Sasha, his eyes expressionless. "Any more questions, and I'll tape your mouth shut."

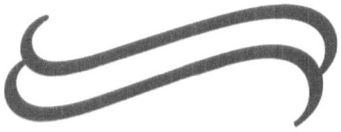

When Hans and Mihai arrived at the apartment building, they found the door wide open. Hans went in first, gun extended. The place stank of vermin, the floor littered with trash. It wasn't until they reached a bedroom that Hans knew Sasha had been here. He spied her barrette on the dirty floor and picked it up.

Just then there was a sound behind them. Hans swung around to see a boy of about ten standing in the doorway. "Ask him if he's seen Sasha," he instructed Mihai. Hans pulled some bills out of his pocket. "Tell him I'll pay for good information."

Mihai began talking with the boy, then translated for Hans. "He says she was just here. A man he's calling the chief put her in a van."

"Ask him to tell me anything he knows. Which way did they head?"

The boy looked at Hans with fear in his eyes, then down at the money in his hand.

"Tell him the chief won't know he talked to me."

Mihai translated. "The boy says he does errands for the chief. He's had to go to a house where there are many women, several blocks from here."

"I'll pay him after he takes us to the house."

Mihai consulted with the boy, who eyed Hans, then agreed.

As they headed out, Hans hoped the boy wasn't leading them on a fruitless trip.

After jerking the van to a stop, Andreas got out and

pulled Sasha out, then rapped hard several times on a black metal door. The door swung open to reveal a burly man in a t-shirt, his biceps covered in tattoos. He eyed Sasha with interest.

"She's mine," said Andreas. "Bring her to the back room. I'll be in soon."

The man grabbed Sasha by the arm and pulled her down a dark hallway lined with closed doors. She could hear women crying and gruff voices. When they arrived at an empty room, the man pushed Sasha inside and shut the door. In the dim light, she could make out a dingy cot and a bucket.

Some time passed, Sasha's nerves jangling every time she heard a noise outside the room. Finally, the door flew open and crashed against the wall. Andreas strutted in. Sasha held her blouse over her breasts as he came to stand before her.

"We have been too lenient with you," he said, his mouth a grim line. "You were living a good life in America. We allowed you to use your nursing skills."

"I was working seven days a week, twelve hours a day for your sister and Dr. Cesero. Or should I say the Russian mafia."

Andreas seemed surprised at Sasha's revelation about Alina. He spit on the floor. "My sister has always been obsessed by wanting too much and has never known when to stop." He glanced around the room, his gaze falling on the cot. Then he started to reach for Sasha when she put her hands out.

"Wait. Where is my mother? I'll do whatever you want, but I need you to release her."

Andreas sniggered and continued advancing toward her. "It's too late for your mother."

At his remark, anger like Sasha had never felt before boiled in her chest and she shoved him forcefully. This seemed to excite him, as he laughed and lunged for her. When he crushed her to him, Sasha's hand came in contact with the gun in the back of his pants. In a split second, she grabbed it and jerked herself backwards, aiming at his chest. "I'll shoot you," she said.

Andreas snorted. "You don't have it in you."

Filled with horror at what her mother must have endured, Sasha pulled the trigger.

Once they arrived at their destination, Hans handed the boy several bills and told him to leave. Then he rapped on the door of the building just as a gunshot rang out from inside. When the doorknob refused to turn, Hans began beating on the door so hard it dented. When it was clear he wasn't getting in, he pulled out his phone and gave it to Mihai. "We're going to have to take our chances with the local police."

Mihai made the call, and within five agonizing minutes, a police car siren sounded in the distance, soon becoming louder. When the car arrived, two officers advanced, shouting in Hungarian.

"Tell them innocent people are being held captive in there," Hans told Mihai, who informed the officers.

They didn't immediately go in, instead called for backup. When they finally forced their way through the door, guns drawn, shouts and shots rang out. In every aching second, Hans prayed Sasha was alright.

Rage foamed in Andrea's eyes as he grasped his shoulder. "You bitch," he cried, advancing toward her.

Sasha's hands trembled while she tried to keep the gun steady. She was gathering the courage to take another shot when shouting erupted outside the room. That distracted her for a millisecond, and Andreas lunged at her, wrestling the gun out of her grasp just as the door kicked open. A police officer ordered him to put the gun down. Instead, Andreas stuck the pistol at Sasha's temple and threatened to shoot. She could feel the blood from Andreas's shoulder wound seeping into the back of her clothing. She knew that with increasing blood loss, his oxygen levels would be sinking. Gathering all her strength, she smacked her head back on his chest, and slid out of his grasp just as a shot from the officer's gun rang out, hitting Andreas in the forehead. As Sasha stood there shaking, Andreas crumpled to the ground, the blood oozing out of his head and onto the floor.

A few minutes later, a Hungarian policewoman guided her through the hallway, where Sasha saw dozens of women being led out. Then the back of a familiar head. Were her eyes playing tricks on her? "*Anya!*" she cried. When the head turned and she met the eyes of her mother, joy surged through Sasha. She pushed her way past several people to run to her. They embraced for a long time, both sobbing and saying that they never thought they'd see one another again. When the tears stopped coming, they pulled apart, and Sasha was surprised to see Hans standing there.

She went to him and looped her arm through his. "*Anya,*

I'd like you to meet someone. This is Hans. He came here from America with me to help you."

Her mother turned to look at Hans, then back at Sasha, questions in her eyes.

"Hans is a doctor," said Sasha.

Her mother's face brightened, and she put out her hand. "It's very nice to meet one of your friends," she said in stilted English.

It was then that Sasha noticed Mihai, standing back, waiting. He came forward, a pensive look on his face.

"Mihai, your mother is here. She was with me a few minutes ago," Sasha's mother told him. "We were separated when we were being led out."

They spent the next several hours in the police station where Sasha's mother and Natalya explained to the police the details of their kidnapping. During this time, she and Hans talked with the Interpol agent.

"Thanks to you, Andreas Bakós is no longer a threat, and we are in the process of rescuing hundreds of women here and in America," said the agent. "We are still working on locating Alina Bakós. She was last seen in Los Angeles boarding a plane for the Virgin Islands. It looks like she expanded the operations in the US with the help of Cesero. The Russian syndicate was paying them for facial reconstruction surgeries of known international criminals and their family members."

Though Sasha should have been shocked at the revelation, when she looked back at all the signs now, it wasn't that surprising. "There was a abdominoplasty patient who went missing before Dr. Cesero was shot. A female," said Sasha. "This was a second surgery for her. The first time we did extensive facial reconstruction work."

The Interpol agent raised her eyebrows. "It would be

good to identify her. I will call the FBI and have them check for DNA evidence at Cesero's office."

"No need," said Sasha. "I have the sheets she bled on."

The Interpol agent smiled. "That makes our jobs a lot easier."

"Alina was holding another Hungarian woman, who I didn't see here today. Her name is Anna," said Sasha. "Has she been located?"

The agent shook her head. "Anna Rosko seems to have disappeared."

## 30

After the police released them, they all went back to Natalya's house so Sasha's mother could collect her things. Though everyone was relieved to have escaped Andreas's clutches, the dark cloud of Anna still being missing permeated the mood. Natalya tried to put on a brave front, but Sasha saw the despair in her eyes. Regret washed through her as she thought about how close Anna had been in the clinic.

When Sasha's mother said goodbye to her friend, Natalya began to cry. Then she brushed away tears as Mihai came to stand next to his mother, placing his arm protectively around her.

Walking up the cracked cement stairs of her mother's apartment a few minutes later, Sasha suddenly felt embarrassed. What would Hans think of the ancient, tired building with its stained linoleum floors that her mother scrubbed but never got clean? As they walked through the threshold, Hans smiled and took Sasha's hand and squeezed it. When he did this, she was reminded of his good-heartedness. He had accepted Sasha for herself, and she trusted he would do the same with her mother.

Once in the main room, Sasha noticed Hans eyeing a pile of mending on a roughhewn table. "My mother did seamstress work for many years," he said.

Sasha must have given him a shocked look because he added, "My parents were immigrants. My mother worked in the LA garment district, and my father in a canning factory."

When Sasha told her mother what he said, her eyes lit up. Then she went to the cupboard and pulled out a bottle of *palinka*, along with three small glasses. She poured them all a drink. As Sasha took a sip of the strong homemade brew, she thought this was as good a time as any for her announcement. "*Anya*, I have news," she told her in Hungarian. "Hans is my husband."

When the words registered, her mother clasped her hands to her chest and tears sprang to her eyes. Then she held up her glass and toasted to them both.

After they finished their celebratory drinks, Sasha made them all cold cut sandwiches. It was a simple meal, but sitting here with Sasha, glowing now that she was safely with her mother, Hans didn't think he'd ever tasted any food more delicious. They talked into the night, Sasha translating and her mother asking questions of Hans about his family and work as a neurosurgeon.

At one point, Hans said, "Why doesn't your mother come to the United States with us? We can have a proper wedding ceremony and invite my mother, too."

When Sasha told her mother, she became very animated, then pushed back her chair and went into the adjoining room, returning with an old pendant on a chain. She showed it to the two of them, then said something to Sasha.

"*Anya* says the pendant belonged to her father, and she wants you to have it. She will be honored to come for the wedding, but in a few months' time when she's been able to talk to her doctors and prepare for the journey."

"Tell her I understand," said Hans. "When she's ready, I'll pay for everything."

Hans got a text then and checked the screen. It was Robert. "Excuse me for a second," he said, then dialed Robert's number.

"Hans, my sources say all has been resolved there. You and Sasha are okay?"

"I am. Sasha's mother is safely home, and Andreas is dead." He paused. "Only one MIA. The young lady who Sasha and I treated at Cesero's clinic."

"We still have no word on Anna. She wasn't spotted with Alina when she fled the country. I'm sorry, old friend, this is the way it goes sometimes. Be grateful you and Sasha and her mother are alive."

"I am extremely grateful. I don't think I'd be talking to you right now if it weren't for your help. I know you do this sort of thing for a living, but I'm happy to go back to medicine. I'm much more comfortable with a scalpel than a gun."

His next call was to arrange for his mother's transport back to Meadowbrook, with a message to let her know he'd be seeing her soon.

Hans and Sasha left Hungary the next morning. At the security check in they showed their real passports. Besides the two alias passports, Helga had made one with the name Sasha Wagner. Inside she had stuck a note that said, "Congratulations!"

As soon as they touched down in Los Angeles, Hans said, "I'm sure you're tired, but I need to go see my mother as soon as possible."

"Let's go right now."

"Are you sure you're up to it?"

"I am tired, but we don't want to keep your mother worrying any longer than necessary."

When they walked into the care facility a few minutes later, Sasha was impressed with the beautiful, clean building. The large entryway featured a giant vase filled with colorful flowers, and the air smelled fresh, like newly washed laundry.

Hans's mother was having lunch, so they headed to the dining room. When they approached the table where a woman sat alone eating a salad, Sasha felt nervous—until she looked up at them with the same kind eyes as her son's. She gave them a welcoming smile, then turned her attention to Hans. "I am so glad to see you are okay. I have many questions for you. But first, who is this lovely woman?" She looked from Hans to Sasha expectantly.

"Mom, this is Sasha, my wife. Sasha, this is my mother, Gretchen."

At the look of surprise that crossed the woman's face, Sasha found herself holding her breath. Then Gretchen said with a smile, "It is very nice to meet you, Sasha, or should I say daughter-in-law. Please sit and have lunch with me. I want to hear all about how you both met. I know you must be a very special woman."

Sasha awoke and stretched as the morning sun streamed in through the condo's bedroom windows. She turned over to run her hand along Hans's pillow, still indented from where he had slept before going in at sunrise to check on patients.

She got out of bed and went into the adjoining bathroom to wash her face and brush her teeth. Today, in just a few hours, she would pick her mother up from the airport. She and Natalya were coming for the wedding ceremony and reception to be held the next day at a local hotel overlooking the ocean. As Sasha brushed through her hair and eyed herself in the mirror, she smiled at her reflection, which seemed to glow. The last two months with Hans, planning their wedding and talking about their future, had been a delightful blur.

Before her mother's arrival, she needed to run to a department store to buy a new nightgown for her wedding night. She had been reading bridal magazines about the customary things to do for a wedding here in America, and apparently, she needed some lingerie.

When she walked into the department store, Sasha felt awkward to look at such beautiful, intimate garments. After bypassing skimpy items and garter belts that made her blush, she chose a calf-length, lavender gown, silky and plain, but with a frill of lace on the bodice. After she paid and was about to leave, a man and woman approached the checkout stand. Sasha glanced up at the sound of the woman's voice and stifled a gasp when she looked at her face. It was Anna! Eyes on the floor, Sasha walked away quickly and went into the adjacent department. Hands shaking, she opened her purse and fished out the FBI agent's card, then dialed her number.

"Agent Sanchez, it's me," she whispered when the woman answered. "I am in Nordstrom's on Santa Monica Boulevard. Anna is here with a man in the lingerie department at the cash register."

"You stay clear," Agent Sanchez ordered. "I'll handle this."

Sasha remained where she was, peeking to see the phone ring and the salesperson answer. She watched as the young woman listened intently, then said, "Okay, thank you." She hung up the phone and continued the purchase.

At one point, the man complained about her slowness. "Can you hurry up?" he said. Sasha detected a Russian accent. Minutes later, several police officers appeared, guns drawn, and surrounded the man and Anna.

"Are you Anna Rosko?" asked one officer.

"Pardon me, officer, I'm afraid you're mistaken," said the man, taking a firm grip of Anna's arm. "This is Madeline, my wife. We're in a terrible hurry. Excuse us."

When Anna appeared to hesitate at his words, Sasha cried out, "Anna, tell them it's you."

Anna's eyes darted from the police, back to the man, as if uncertain what to do. Then she wrenched her arm from his grasp. "My name is Anna Rosko," she said, her voice quavering. "Please help me. I'm being held against my will." As she said this, the man pushed her toward the counter and tried to run, but two officers tackled and subdued him.

"It's you, the nurse," said Anna, eyes wide when Sasha approached her.

"I am the nurse who cared for you. My name is Sasha Farkas. Your mother and my mother are friends."

Anna's face flooded with relief and happiness. "Is my mother okay?"

Sasha smiled. "Your mother is fine. She'll be so happy to see you."

"I never thought I would see her again," said Anna, her legs appearing to give way slightly.

Sasha reached out to steady her. "She's on a flight right now from Hungary to Los Angeles. The plane arrives in a couple of hours."

Anna put her hand to her mouth as tears filled her eyes.

Agent Sanchez walked up then. "Good job, Sasha, fast thinking," she said. Then she turned to Anna. "We need to talk to you at headquarters, Ms. Rosko. The man you're accusing of holding you captive, Maxim Petrov, is a wealthy Russian expatriate, who owns a shipping line here in Los Angeles. You need to make your official statement so we can get this guy. I also think it would be good to speak to our psychologist after the trauma you've endured."

"Do you want me to go with you?" asked Sasha.

Anna shook her head. "No, please go get my mother and tell her I'm okay." She grasped Sasha's hand. "Thank you. You saved my life."

Sasha swallowed, a well of emotion filling her throat. "I'm sorry I didn't do anything when you were in the clinic."

Anna shook her head. "There was nothing you could do. All that matters now is my mother and I will be reunited."

After Anna left with Agent Sanchez, Sasha dialed Hans's number.

"Yes, love," he answered. "Did you find what you were looking for?"

"Much more," said Sasha. "I found Anna."

Hans was silent for a moment. "I would say you've got to be kidding, but I know you wouldn't kid about that. That's wonderful news—for everyone."

"Yes," said Sasha, feeling her heart swell with joy as she walked out of the store and looked up into the brilliant blue sky.

# EPILOGUE

**Sasha's and Hans's stories are complete, but Savannah Sanchez's is just beginning....**

Savannah Sanchez's heels echoed in the FBI headquarters' parking garage as she headed for her car. It had been a long day, and she was ready for a pinot grigio and a hot bath. She pushed the keypad on the side of her car and opened the door and got in, then slipped her gun out of its holster and set it on the seat next to her. Keys in the ignition, she was about to turn on the engine when someone opened the back door and slid into the seat behind her. She jumped and turned to see a person with a black ski mask, wielding a gun.

"Eyes forward," said the muffled voice. "Put your hands on the steering wheel."

Savannah wound her hands on the wheel and glanced out of the corner of her eye at her gun. Her visitor would get a shot off before she even had a chance to reach for it.

"I won't hurt you unless I have to," said the voice behind the mask. "I just need you to listen."

"What do you want?" asked Savannah.

"Justice," said the voice. Savannah heard what sounded like paper rustling and the person handed her a manila envelope over her left shoulder.

She took the envelope. "What's in here?"

"Something you need to see."

"If this contains ricin, I'm going to make sure you get a good dose, too," warned Savannah.

"This is a different kind of deadly," said the voice. "Open the envelope."

Savannah lifted the clasp and pulled up on the flap, then reached in and removed some photographs.

"Is this a joke?" she asked, flipping through the photos, each of various orchids.

"No," her assailant's voice became agitated. "Unless you call millions of dollars of contraband a joke."

"I don't think I've seen orchids with such beautiful petals and extravagant colors. Are they rare?"

"The rarest, Agent Sanchez."

"You obviously know who I am. You should also know the FBI doesn't have jurisdiction over plants. If someone is stealing rare or endangered orchids, you need to call Fish and Wildlife."

"The FBI does have jurisdiction over murder."

"You're telling me someone was killed over these orchids? That sounds highly unlikely."

"More than someone has been killed," the voice said. "There's a contact name in the envelope. He will tell you more."

Savannah opened the envelope again and spotted a card at the bottom. She reached in to retrieve it as her captor jumped out of the car. Tossing the envelope and picking up her gun, she hopped out of the car and chased after her mystery guest yelling, "Stop! FBI!" But when she got to the parking garage exit and raced out onto the sidewalk to glance both ways, there was no one in sight.

Read Savannah's story in *Discovered Transgressions*.

# A NOTE FOR YOU

Dear Reading Gem,

Thanks for spending time with me, Hans and Sasha! While each of the books in the Discovered Truth Series can be read as a standalone, it's fun to experience the progression and get to know the characters. The series progresses as minor characters introduced in each book become main characters in subsequent books. It's exciting to see what they'll do next!

The Discovered Truth series features complex, gutsy women and equally complicated, charismatic men who find themselves immersed in dangerous and intriguing modern-day challenges, such as human trafficking, drug smuggling, organ theft, national security threats, and identity theft. When the heroine and hero meet, worlds collide and sparks fly, kindling unforgettable romance and intrigue.

Thanks again and talk soon!

# STAY ENLIGHTENED

Dear Reading Gem, thanks for reading! Let's stay in touch.

Join my weekly newsletter Julie's Reading Gems here. You get a **free prequel novella** to the series for signing up. There are also weekly giveaways and contests to win free books in the series.

You can also find me on my website at https://www.juliebawdendavis.com/fiction, email me at Julie@JulieBawdenDavis.com, and follow me on Amazon.

**Escape to Unforgettable Romance and Intrigue...**

# YOUR OPINION MATTERS

If you liked this book, please leave a review on Amazon, GoodReads, BookBub, or all three. If you don't wish to leave a review or don't have time, please leave a rating. Every star helps!

# BOOKS IN THE DISCOVERED TRUTH SERIES

*Discovered Beginnings:*
(FREE at https://www.juliebawdendavis.com/fiction)
*Discovered Secrets*
*Discovered Memories*
*Discovered Indiscretions*
*Discovered Liaisons*
*Discovered Betrayal*
*Discovered Denial*
*Discovered Distractions*
*Discovered Deception*
*Discovered Lies*
*Discovered Vengeance*
*Discovered Redemption*
*Discovered Obsession*
*Discovered Transgressions*
*Discovered Suspicion*
*Discovered Escape*
*Discovered Promises*
*Discovered Cover-up*
*Discovered Intentions*

**Box Sets**

The Discovered Truth Series Box Set Books 1-4

The Discovered Truth Series Box Set Books 5-8

The Discovered Truth Series Box Set Books 9-12

The Discovered Truth Series Box Set Books 13-16

www.ingramcontent.com/pod-product-compliance
Lightning Source LLC
Chambersburg PA
CBHW022122170626
46808CB00002B/812